A WORKING WOMAN

A WORKING WOMAN

Elvira Navarro
Translated by Christina MacSweeney

TWO LINES
PRESS

Originally published as: *La trabajadora* by Elvira Navarro
© 2014 by Elvira Navarro
Published in coordination with Casanovas & Lynch Agencia Literaria S.L.

Translation © 2017 by Christina MacSweeney

Two Lines Press
582 Market Street, Suite 700, San Francisco, CA 94104
www.twolinespress.com

ISBN 978-1-931883-65-8

Library of Congress Control Number: 2017940025

Cover design by Gabriele Wilson
Cover photo by Adam Voorhes / Gallery Stock
Typeset by Sloane | Samuel

Printed in the United States of America

1 3 5 7 9 10 8 6 4 2

This project is supported in part by an award from
the National Endowment for the Arts.

ART WORKS.
arts.gov

I recognize the universe in every face, be it beautiful or ugly, sublime or grotesque, exalted or common; I have no illusions with regard to what is ridiculous, comic, or anodyne: at the right distance, everything is. In contrast, for you, who claim to be a delirious realist, behind literature there is only literature.

LUIS MAGRINYÀ

PART ONE

FABIO

[*This story is based on what Susana told me about her madness. I've added some of my own reactions, but to be honest, they are very few. It goes without saying her narrative was more chaotic:*]

I'd just come back to Madrid, the Internet didn't exist, and I had to depend on newspapers. I'd focused all my desire on finding someone to suck my pussy while I was having my period, and the moon was full. For no particular reason. I think madness had hidden there, in that extreme but also tiny ambition, like swallowing a centipede tossed in the salad. In the beginning, I didn't give it much thought, unless I had a newspaper in front of me open to the section of men and women hatching three-line conspiracies; then the mania would grab hold of me, and I'd call and turn up any old how for the date. I kept a record of my periods, and would ask for the next meeting to be on the full moon, in my apartment. Most of them responded with a nervous negative, and the reason wasn't that they considered my proposition peculiar; it was because I blurted it out as if I was playing Russian roulette. And because of my bulging red-faced blondeness, my coming-apart-at-the-seams way of speaking, and a pair of eyes whose futile, terrifying ship-wreck said it all. I know what my eyes were like; with the fogged clarity of my five senses, I used to measure the level of absurdity in my dumb, doped-up expressions, seemingly more attentive than I was actually capable of, my face toss-ing around on convulsive currents, creating unexpected gri-maces. They all looked at me in disgust, and when added to the fact I was ugly, and clearly mad, my proposition didn't help matters. Don't get it into your head I cared. Yes, I was careful about the venue, and in the end did the rounds of all the bars in Huertas that had a coffee-shop ambience, with hands cradling hot cups in the dim light. I liked to con-template the street through a window that linked the cold outside to the patina of dry heat within, that muffled-up heat of water on top of radiators and cigarette smoke, when we all still smoked. I call it a coffee-shop ambience because I didn't want the venues to actually be coffee shops. Old ladies used to go to coffee shops for afternoon snacks, and in their eyes I was always guilty. I'm talking about the times when coffee shops oozed women in mourning with backcombed hair. Those sixty-year-olds couldn't forgive the flat, reheated croissant dunked in Nescafé at 6 p.m., and I used to arrange to meet the advertisers at seven. I managed to find a slightly unwelcoming green-walled bar that always had a table available by the window. I wasn't particularly interested in the age of the men I arranged to meet, or their appearance, just as long as they didn't have stains on their clothes, long grimy nails, or bits of salad stuck between their teeth. That wasn't normally the case; they inevitably turned up looking neat to the first date. On the second, given my requirement, some didn't make the same effort. Then I'd see the thought draped on their bodies: Why bother for her? If that's her idea, well… But they still used to try it one more time, you never know your luck. They wanted me to take them up to my attic, saying: Oh of course, my pleasure, no, ladies first. But I'd already seen their faces. People who have lost respect for themselves soon lose respect for others. I'll be honest, very few came back for a second date. Just the ones who'd been single for so long that their jackets were a testament to their pasta etiquette. That's what I meant about the stains. Desperation doesn't usually go that far. Madness is frightening, and the men used to push back their chairs as soon as I brought out my calendar and pointed a bright red finger to the phase of the moon, as if summoning the tides. The ones with a bit more delicacy waited long enough to finish their beers before they left. Finding someone who would agree to fulfill my desire got to be so important that, when I realized not a single one of the men who didn't frighten me was willing to consider it, I moved on to women. I've never liked them much because it's like kissing myself, but for what I wanted, they were just as useful. Well, almost just as useful. And they didn't find it shocking, even if they did think it a pretty unusual first course. I cottoned to the fact that responding to someone else's requirements made me feel less powerful, so I began placing my own ads. They'd taken me off Risperdal and put me on lithium by then: I'd been recategorized from schizophrenic to bipolar. Lithium has fewer side effects, and that meant I could follow a conversation. A part of my energy leaked away in the placement of the weekly announcements—addressed to both men and women, because I'd learned my lesson by that stage—in all the newspapers. Now, when I look back, I don't think I wanted to replicate my pre-drug madness, just find a simple obsession that would keep me amused. I had nothing to do at that time. And when I say nothing, I mean, read my lips: NOTHING [*Susana enunciated the two syllables, almost spitting out the first*], and you can't imagine how depressing it is for reality, or your head, to be a piece of dull, broken glass thrown on the sidewalk. That objective centered me. It gave me a kind of Amazonian air, and the illusion I had a compass in my hand. I also placed an ad directed at gays: "Heterosexual woman seeks homosexual men." After six months, I'd lost all hope, because I hadn't managed to find anyone to suck my pussy while I was having my period, on a second date, when the moon was full. I hadn't even found anyone I liked. The lesbians who answered my ad all looked like dykes: short hair, broad shoulders, volleyball-champion arms. I'd never in my life dated so many people, but, like I said, having an objective gave me stability. I'm not even sure now if it had to do with sex, because I spent most of my time in a haze. If the other person talked a lot, and I had to listen, I used to fall asleep. And when I woke, there'd be no one there.

Then one fall day, Fabio turned up. He was Mexican, though no one would have guessed it, given his Irish looks. I had kind of an obsession with anything blond. [*She made a vague gesture, like a Thompson's gazelle lying in wait for a camera in a wildlife documentary. I was about to say something, but...*] One day my psychoanalyst said I was looking for the child I used to be in all the blond men I fell in love with. A second shrink, Jungian this time, came out with the idea that I worshipped the Aryan race. [*I looked at the floor; if Susana wanted me to believe her, these ridiculous observations weren't helping, but on the other hand, the part of me that curiously observed and envied her freedom in constructing an image of herself gave a faint signal of delight. I was accustomed to her exaggerations, even to her lies, although not when they were so out of proportion. The fact that her fantasy was so over the top gave me hope of being able to separate the wheat from the chaff, and even that Susana might tell me what I was anxious to hear; something made important only by the greed of deferral. On the other hand, being doped up myself made me doubtful, as if what I was hearing could be absorbed naturally into my cells without chemical intervention.*] Fabio replied to my ad for homosexuals. He presented himself as a tracker of what was behind those announcements. He knew what requests were hidden there, even if they were brief. He could smell them. He spent his whole day smelling newspapers and magazines. According to him, the source of the scent lingered on them. [*It may be I fell asleep for a few seconds at that point, like a student in the front row whose eyelids droop for just a moment because her desire not to be caught by the teacher is taking a nap. Perhaps I used sleep as a way of excusing Susana, or forgiving myself. Suddenly her nerve began to annoy me. I passed from enthusiasm to suspecting she was taking advantage of my drug-induced stupidity. Or maybe I didn't really understand her, and she was talking in that delirious way because her medication hadn't taken effect yet.*]

Did I miss something essential when I dropped off for those few moments?] To give me some idea of his sensory abilities, he asked if I was aware that words have colors. Hope, he said, was blue. A car falling off a bridge was white, and if there was water under the bridge, it was the color of downpours in what was once known as Indochina. And the same thing happened with smells: they all gave off a subtle aroma only to be found inside our brains, not on the outside. He wasn't certain if physical objects corresponded to this model, he said, but he couldn't find any other way to explain the stuff about his nose to me. Everything I'm telling you happened before we had cell phones, and we used to record calls on those automatic answering machines. I loved the beep, and then my voice on the cassette—I always tried to make it sound husky and sensual, like in movies, but it never worked. You know what my voice is like: it's as if I'm wiping my vocal chords with a Kleenex. It was a Tuesday, I'd been taking my anxiety out for a walk in the Sabatini Gardens, and when I got back to my hole in the Plaza Mayor, I found the red light on the machine blinking overtime. It was always like that, because I put in ads every day. Despite the messages being exasperatingly similar, that time, when I saw the light flickering in the darkness like the eye of the Devil, I had a premonition, and ran to the answering machine like one of those heroines in made-for-TV movies. I'd never before had that sense of being so happy in taking the leading role. Fabio was the last to speak, after five men between thirty and fifty who sounded as if they were chewing on licorice sticks, and two twenty-something women with difficult-to-pin-down interests. Just like Fabio with his sense of smell, after six months of meeting strangers I'd only heard before on the answering machine, I could tell almost everything about them from their voices. I never hung up, just let them go on murmuring their desires and telephone numbers; later on I used to listen to them compulsively, over and over, until I started to distrust my intuition, which always told me: No, there's nothing for you here, Susana. My intuition was so devastatingly accurate, I had to crush it. This time I listened, and was alone with a voice stammering: You smell of blood. I turned up at the bar feeling frightened; at the third table on the left, always reserved for me, sat Fabio with his white skin that, in the oblique light, looked gray.

"How old are you?" I asked.

He was so short. I thought I must have at least half a decade on him. If he'd told me he was playing hooky from school, I wouldn't have blinked an eyelid. But Fabio gave a sigh, and I understood; there was nothing adolescent—not even postadolescent—in that sigh; anyway, he accompanied it with an identification document giving his age as twenty-six.

"Same as me."

"It says that in your ad."

I'd suddenly forgotten all about the blood. I'd also forgotten why I'd agreed to meet a person who looked like that—as if I'd ever seen the others' faces. Fabio resembled Mr. Galindo, the dwarf from *The Martian Chronicles*, that late-night talk show no one ever missed back then. [*I couldn't help but laugh, imagining Fabio, and gave Susana all the credit for that, although "credit" isn't exactly the right word. What I mean is I stopped speculating about her intentions, maybe because I found her story unsettling, and after that I was just thinking about him. What's more, if I was going to let her continue talking, there was no point in getting defensive. Fine, I told myself, just watch where's she's heading. And if she doesn't head anywhere, you can cut her off. But, no, I wouldn't have the courage to do that.*] The thing is that, for long moments, I had no idea what was going on; I just sat across from Fabio and let the side effects of the lithium take over. They're like viruses and bacteria: they invade you when your defenses are low. My vision went blurry, I started having palpitations, felt I needed to piss, and an unpleasant sweat was trickling down between my breasts. When I touched it, I realized that the sweat was slimy, but my sense of touch was probably affected too.

"Excuse me, I have to go to the restroom."

I could hardly manage even a few drops. I splashed water on my face, considered taking a couple of anxiolytics, but discounted that idea because I wasn't sure if they would counteract the effects of the lithium. When I came back, I was as white as Fabio. And I was also in some way just as short as him, even though I'm six foot. I knew he had me hooked.

"My mother didn't let me grow," he told me.

I was in no mood for guessing games or metaphors, so I just said, "What?"

"I mean I'm not even five feet tall because my mother didn't want me to grow into an adult."

"But you are an adult."

"You've seen my ID."

"Yeah."

I still couldn't believe it. In spite of his dwarfism, Fabio had long bones, which right from the start made him a contradiction. It was like the effect glass figurines have: they always seem bigger than they really are. I don't enjoy feeling three heads taller than a man, and I felt so conscious of my height in his presence, I ordered a whiskey on the rocks to stop myself from thinking about my proportions. He opted for an instant decaf.

"So?"

I was filling space, nothing more. Like I just told you, I'd forgotten my objective. All I knew was my reason for meeting around a hundred other people over the course of the previous months wasn't the same reason that had me there at that moment.

"I know you want me to suck your pussy during your period, and if possible, when you're bleeding most heavily, which is when the moon is full."

Here I should say something like: I looked at him in astonishment. I allowed the whiskey to take effect without worrying I'd forget things, because I knew Fabio was going to remind me about them. That afternoon, we talked about his life, mine, and—due to some intricacies of the conversation that are hard to reproduce—how off-putting we found the El Almendro nougat commercial. [*I remembered that commercial, remembered seeing it from the warmth of a green sofa with scratchy upholstery, my feet like a rubber doll cuddling a circular electric brazier, and the sweet smell of nougat, oranges, candies with cherry brandy filling. I think what first appeared on the TV screen was the silhouette of a village, glowing in the light of Christ's coming. That light was kaleidoscopic, it might break*]

down into fleeting images, but they took up residence in percep-
tion because of their familiar connotations: wood piled up in car-
ports standing next to false doors, or chicken runs; the comforting
smoke from chimneys lulling household gods; the snow falling
with the promptness of one of those glass spheres whose snow-
flakes produce miniature, manageable beauties that can be put on
a vanity table. A boy rushed into a room that had the proportions
of a kitsch fantasy, because that town, whose silhouette made you
think of Extremadura or Cádiz, didn't have wooden tables with
heaters installed underneath or whitewashed walls, but those
large La Moraleja villa sort of windows, a fir tree, the sort of
hearth you see in an American movie. Then the mother came in,
her hair rigid with spray, her dress buttoned up to the neck and
an air of religious services, hats, and face powder. I don't know
how many years they showed that commercial for, or maybe they
made a new one each year; I haven't watched TV since going
to college. And due to that commercial, whenever I visited my
hometown in Andalusia to celebrate Christmas, I always had the
impression something wasn't there—something just out of reach
the grown-ups hadn't done. It seemed to me reasonable to express
a certain sense of disappointment.] Was it El Almendro or El
Lobo nougat? I get them mixed up. I haven't watched TV for
ages. Fabio told me he hadn't been back home for Christmas
since his father died. He'd been in Spain for seven years, his
mother lived in Santander, and if he was going to spend his
dough, he'd prefer to do it on a trip to some latitude where
Christmas didn't exist. There was no such thing as budget
travel in the eighties. He was very insistent about how much
money you spent on long journeys. And he hadn't gotten
citizenship yet. But thanks to his sense of smell, he did have

a good job. He was employed by the National Intelligence Center to smell murderers and terrorists in letters and other documents. The information revolution was just beginning, and he was very worried: his sense of smell didn't work with screens. He also got paid for letting two groups of neuroscientists in the Research Council investigate him. And the people at the Grupo Hepza, which looks into paranormal phenomena, did experiments on him. [*Heard from my cloud: the consistency of dreams, but I'd swear I wasn't dreaming. I don't think I've made it clear that it was the mixture of antidepressants and anxiolytics that made me sleepy. Susana's story was weird enough to keep me awake, but sometimes tiredness got the better of me. However, I'm positive this didn't affect my hearing, and even when I was almost dropping off, her words fixed themselves in my memory, because I have a clear recollection of them, with scarcely any gaps. I was motivated by irritation and confusion, by what I'd have liked to inquire into, but which remained in the shadows; I didn't close my eyes on more than three occasions, and those blackouts lasted no longer than seconds. Susana didn't notice.*] And he was there in the bar because he was willing to do what I wanted. It was, he said, one of his favorite sexual practices, something impossible to do with men. He reiterated that he was homosexual.

"I've only got a single requirement: I want a mirror on one side."

Like I said, I had an attic apartment in the Plaza Mayor. Now I think my living conditions in that attic were precursors of what has happened to housing over the last twenty years. I refused to inhabit a larger, more comfortable space because of my thing about money. It was one of the manias that got their hooks into me after my psychotic episode: I'd never find a job that paid enough to live on. And though I still had my inheritance, I thought it might run out any day, figures in the red while I was putting on my shoes and taking my lithium, so that's why I rented an attic where you could only stand upright in the center. The toilet and shower were in full view. The owner said if I wanted partitions, he'd increase the rent, which was ridiculously low, especially compared to what we pay now. I could have rented a five-bedroom house in the Salamanca neighborhood for the price of my room in your apartment [*I looked away*], but I was terrified, and so accepted living that way, not being able to go to the bathroom when I had a visitor. I could also have bought a proper apartment, or even a rundown building. I'm trying to say I wasn't rational about money. And buying a rundown building would have meant I had to work, which in turn would have meant I couldn't keep such close track of the people who answered my ads. And that was the basis of my life then. I kept it secret from my psychiatrist and psychotherapist. I was afraid they'd disapprove. [*I thought about my own new psychiatrist, about how people believe shrinks are no use, but they do have a special talent for interpreting gestures, hesitations, omissions, unsuccessful acts.*] For a year and a half, I was incapable of breaking my routine of medication and ads, and so also unable to look for work or sign up for a college course, which is exactly what I did when I felt better. The thing is that Fabio landed in my attic one Saturday on a full moon, on the second day of my cycle, and then, when I was lying on the floor, and he was at the point of getting to the nectar, I closed my legs. I suddenly saw clearly that it wouldn't come free, that it wasn't the sort of sexual activity he'd like. When I closed my legs, I accidentally cracked Fabio in the jaw: he cried out in pain. After he stopped howling, he told me he had a bone condition that affected his mandible. He lay there for a while on one corner of the mattress, naked, tiny, and very still. He'd put on my bathrobe because it was cold, and instead of him sucking me off we fucked. My orgasm was so intense I felt faint. We did it many more times over the following months, despite him being gay, and in theory not liking women, just as I didn't like men who were that puny. You had to admire the fact that, though my libido was sluggish—almost nonexistent—because of the medication, when Fabio touched me it was as if his fingertips contained some kind of potion, and that's how it was for as long as our relationship lasted. When we finished, he'd walk to the window, as if he wanted to escape, and I'd go back to not feeling anything, and that made me wonder about the nature of my desire. If the memory I have of sex with him didn't refloat my desire, what was it that made me open the door to him at seven every evening? Why had I stopped taking my daily constitutionals in the Sabatini Gardens when they did me so much good? The year before I met Fabio, the authorities had decided to abolish daylight savings, so the evenings were shorter, which explains why, in spite of the heat, people were still using duvets, and why in the tree-shaded darkness of the palace gardens the buckles of leather jackets glinted in the half light. Leather and wide belts were in fashion then. Remember? Of course, it was a really strange phenomenon, but my life was already weird enough, and it was no consolation to know that, in the middle of August, the capital of Spain was behaving as if it was suffering a rainy spring. Just like you now [*I looked away again; I was aware of how closely Susana had observed my habits, and I felt as if she'd started unbuttoning my blouse*], something in my nervous system was compelling me to be on the move, especially at night, and that movement wasn't simply something my tense muscles needed; it was as if the day that was walled in by my attic and my head was seeking the breadth of open spaces. I'd walk along Arenal to Ópera, and from there to the Palacio Real, where I allowed my eyes to linger on glimmers so distant and fragile they seemed like fairy lights. Beyond the Paseo de Extremadura and Carabanchel, the residential areas were still made up of buildings that seemed to be apologizing for themselves, and the streets weren't as well lit as they are now. If I concentrated hard enough on moonless nights, I lost all sense of distance. The lights of Somosaguas became twinkles scattered along the hillside, just like the ranchos in Caracas. Have you been to Caracas? Imagining I was somewhere else, or thinking of childhood journeys in the car with my parents and siblings, gave me a kind of gloomy tranquility, as if I'd bottled myself up in a boring but welcoming vacuum. [*This was the first time Susana mentioned her parents and siblings; I managed to look as if I hadn't noticed, which was a waste of effort.*] Then I'd go down to the Sabatini Gardens, where I set about brushing my hands along the turgidity of the boxwoods, the thorns of the rose bushes without roses, the dry black soil, and then, if I was feeling daring, the hair and long-sleeved tracksuit tops of passersby. I'd be wearing a red leather bomber jacket, and could feel the sweat pouring down my back. I remember the few babies being breastfed by mothers all had little hats. Sometimes there were concerts, and you could hear balalaikas, didgeridoos, and Movida groups; on those evenings, I'd pass through the crowd and the music with a degree of longing for the sounds of crickets and harvest bugs, and especially for silence, because that was also essential if I was going to get back to my attic with a sensation of space: the sound field. I could only experience a wide sound field if there was a significant amount of silence seeping strangely out of the flowerbeds, with moths flying noiselessly so as not to disturb the dreams of the queen ants. The way I see it, a lot of noise, a lot of voices, produce the same sensation as canned laughter, and there's a reason why they call it canned and not, for example, stored. I'd sit next to the artificial pond, with its timid but definite dampness rising to evoke great lakes, and look at the statues, even now I don't know who they represent, but in any case they act as guardians of the night, creators of those boxwood mazes it was impossible to get lost in. Not even children could lose their way among those leafy walls. I don't know if it's all still the way I remember; don't know if parks change. Contemplating almond and monkey-puzzle trees isn't the way I learn.

During the day, I didn't think about Fabio. I carried on with my routine of putting ads in the newspapers and listening out for the calls, attentive to the voices on the answering machine's tiny cassette. I started a collection, because something had to be done with those voices if I wasn't going to arrange to date them. What better than listening to them three times a day, enjoying the possibilities they presented? Pressing play was also a way of putting myself on guard, as, in the beginning, I didn't really believe in Fabio. And what else could I do with that drug-induced lethargy, and having spent two delirious weeks in a psychiatric clinic, and six months arranging to meet strangers so they'd suck my pussy while I was having my period? As the weeks passed, and the tiny grasshopper's lovemaking settled into a docile pattern, the voices began to sound different, much more attractive. I started to get attached to them, not out of mere curiosity, or fear of having nothing to do during the long mornings, but because I suddenly couldn't manage without what they suggested: the promise of perfect bodies, a tone that seemed to belong to the person destined to understand me, love me, and feel himself loved by me in the way he'd always imagined, which would never happen now because Fabio was dropping by at seven every evening, that is to say, at the exact same hour as my dates at the Huertas bar. I didn't owe him anything, or at least that's what I told myself, but I didn't go any further. Sometimes I'd wait for him in my bathrobe, having just taken a shower. It didn't occur to me to use soap; I don't like odorless sex, and neither did Fabio. He never missed our date and, while he wasn't in the habit of saying anything tender to me, and even talked about the men he slept with, he seemed wrapped in sadness, and I know there was nostalgia in his eyes, anticipation of loss, and that anticipation sometimes pained him. Even though I didn't feel very much for him, I appreciated his daily visits and the regular sex, something that hadn't been part of my life for a long time. Before that, I'd been fucking in bathrooms for fear the men who came on to me in the club would repent in the taxi home. Regular sex stopped me from being obsessed with sex, and it was a shame I didn't think of anything special to do with that time. I could have set myself to any task without getting distracted. It's also true that the impression of not loving him kept me hooked on the voices, and that before Fabio I'd theorized less about them. But doubt had set in. Why didn't I think about my lover? Why was I so detached? Was detachment good or bad? Maybe it was the medication blocking any strong emotion that made me unsure of what I was feeling. I sometimes tried talking about it with Fabio, but he shied away from putting into words anything he thought would hurt him. I think he had a blind faith in facts and routine, and believed he could win out by not failing me for a single day. He also knew the kind of movies I liked—then, as now, that was almost everything—and would sometimes bring videotapes for us to watch together in bed. From time to time I forced him to go out to the gardens with me, and then he felt even shorter than ever, and wouldn't say a single word. He had such a complex about me being three heads taller than him that he froze, and apparently he'd never been to a park before. I once took him to a restaurant, and he sat there all hunched up, sniffing the menu, because the only thing that made him feel he was on safe ground was being able to tell me how the Asturian chef was feeling when he wrote it. I used to encourage him to talk about his work. I imagined it must be interesting to sniff out murderers and terrorists, but Fabio had a really boring way of telling things. The tone of his voice was like an echo in a ceramic pot, and he was always constructing interminable analogies to help me understand, to a depth we never plumbed, how crucial certain investigations were. He'd get tangled up in complicated State strategies, talking about them in enormous detail until he noticed how bored I was. Then he'd feel hurt. I'd feel sorry for him, and offer to let him spend the night, though I wasn't playing fair in that, because the offer was based on guilt, and, to be honest, some nights what I wanted to do was read, not fuck or sleep beside anyone.

Fabio told me he often asked himself how a pint-sized body could have extraordinary abilities, and had come to the furious conclusion that the greatest power lay in paradox. He could make use of the instantaneous excitement his touch produced in others to sleep with anyone he wanted, but that ended up being so easy there was no fun in it, and he preferred to show himself as he was first, the way he did with me. I didn't tell him that, in my case, he'd had an advantage because he was offering to do something no one else would do. When I think about Fabio these days, I know he's the person who has loved me most, and just as I was, with all that flab he knew how to enjoy; with my butt like a barrel and my kitchen-table legs, and all the edginess of my personality—I suppose the medication softened those edges, though never to the point of eradication—every one of my facial expressions, my freckles, my pale complexion, and the threads of spittle in the corners of my mouth, a for-the-time-being that was more hopeless that anyone else's for-the-time-being, because I had no hope that anything better than what was happening could happen, and I didn't even want what was happening. I only considered the possibility of those kind of big hopes when I was listening to the voices on the answering machine, but as I said, I didn't think there was much chance they would become reality for me. I'm not looking for pity—I'm just saying all this to make the contradictions in my story clear.

We very quickly established a routine. The first thing was always going to bed; then I'd make dinner in the small kitchen that was so awkward to work in: I usually opted for salad and fried hot dogs. We ate the sausages with our fingers; sometimes my conscience rebelled against ingesting so much fat every day, and then I'd buy the soya kind. Fabio never noticed the difference, which seemed odd to me, given his powerful sense of smell. Perhaps he didn't want to mention it. He'd sit on the bed—it was a mattress on the floor—flicking through magazines, but really spying on me, recording my awkwardness on his retina. Maybe what Fabio saw was clear and precise, like an old print: my hands opening a can of tuna, the golden sunflower oil shining on my fingertips, my tongue licking the oil, conscious of the futility of the gesture, because after the oil from the can came the olive oil forming a creamy scum on the outside of the pourer. I've always known exactly what I have in my kitchen. I can't bear disorganization there, as you're well aware. [*I was indeed, but I'd already disordered our kitchen, and she hadn't noticed.*] I don't want to stray off point: I was saying Fabio used to watch my curved back, my clenched buttocks like projectiles—they're my allies now, but then were way over the top. He'd watch all my different postures out of the corner of his eye, and I was just as conscious that his indolence was a pretense, because otherwise I would have felt hurt. We watched each other too much, placed too much importance on each other's reactions. To remedy this situation, he tried concentrating on matters that had nothing to do with me. He'd plug in headphones and listen to major-league soccer games. The commentary was only audible when someone scored a goal. I'd hum to relieve the monotony. There were nights when, after sex, we didn't look at each other again, although that didn't seem to affect the covert attention we paid each other.

One day I stopped pretending. To be honest, I'm not really certain I'd planned it. I'd been strict about our privacy for a few months, and by the time May came around, everything was making me uneasy. What if the people who called after seven didn't try again in the morning? At first, when Fabio arrived, I disconnected the telephone so my meetings with him weren't disturbed by it ringing with enticing but exasperating insistence; the relative novelty of my dates with Fabio meant I didn't mind missing the calls. But after that day, as my belief I was losing out on something grew, instead of unplugging the cord, what I did was turn down the volume on the telephone and the answering machine. That way, all the voices were taped. This involved the minimum of interruption: the click of the record button automatically switching on, and the poltergeist sound of the tape running, like the creaking of the old wooden beams and dried-out parquet when we laid on the floor. Did I say the bed was a mattress on the floor? There was no room for anything else. We were very close to the answering machine, to the jittery record button, to the blinking red eye stuffed full with messages. I eventually covered it with a black dust cloth. And to hide what I'd done, I started to put on music, which mingled with the voices of the tourists who went to the San Ginés chocolate shop to dunk churros. We never mentioned the fact that I continued to place the ads with the peculiar request Fabio had already satisfied on nights with and without a full moon. Sometimes I thought about him going through the newspapers from Monday to Sunday, and coming across the ad, with my repetitive, hurtful words, and I could see his face fall as he imagined a morning routine not dissimilar to the one I had with him later in the day, but with another man, with a lot of other men, maybe with a woman. Who knows if he thought I went to the bar in Huertas alone, without having arranged to meet anyone, because I'd often told him I missed that outing, not for the meetings, but because of the vacuum between them. What I'd been exploring during that time was the simple, but equally mysterious emptiness I was projecting onto the future, that "specter of thought." His nose must have told him I wasn't meeting anyone, but he couldn't help being suspicious, because smell is only an indication. And deep down, Fabio was jealous, so attempting any clarification was a waste of time.

When May came around, with the addition of a heat wave—an explosion without the consolation of night—I had an indefinable but definite sense of unease: the machine needed me; the light, blinking with a new frenzy, held a message I had to listen to that very moment. One night Fabio, who could usually read my mind, turned up the volume so we could listen to the voice of an old man, a deceptive voice saying, Hey angel, how much for a date with me? I'll pay for anything you want. My phone number is

333–4119. I relaxed ipso facto and turned down the volume. That night, I didn't give another thought to the telephone; and I was also calm the next night, but on the third, and the fourth and fifth, it was me who turned up the volume. On the sixth, I didn't even respect our daily coitus; when the phone rang for a second time and a woman's voice spoke, Fabio's hard-on wilted. It was unreasonable for me to get annoyed, but I did. Or rather, I became aware of the potential my annoyance had for allowing me to do what I really wanted: listen to the messages in Fabio's presence without feeling guilty. And in addition to that, there's a third issue I haven't mentioned: I'd gotten accustomed to the answering machine starting up early in the morning, and interrupting my dreams with voices. Although many hours closed in by the darkness, and the answering machine with its buttons at the ready reminded me of the Columbian room where my hallucinations had been conceived, the fact is I only ever received two or three calls in the early hours, normally from drunken men; their slurred, foul-mouthed calls scared me, but never enough to stop me from listening to them. Thanks to those voices, I had the impression the people who were lining up to get into my apartment via the machine were ghosts. That idea came from being half asleep when I heard them. I'd feel cold breath running over my body; but even then I didn't want to discount the possibility of experiencing something from the other side. I thought I'd given up believing in spirits forever, but there was a sensation, sometimes very distinct, of a ghost coming out of the answering machine. In my drowsy state, I seemed to understand the power and inevitability of the conversations, and also of miracles. A Lazarus-stand-up-and-walk sort of logic. When Fabio started sleeping over, something that happened more frequently as June came around, there was absolutely no way I could justify the phone waking us three or four times a night. Like I said, at that hour it was almost always men who showed an interest in my limp-lettuce words. Some called, and then hung up when they got the answering machine. I've always thought they called back, because after the machine clicked off, hardly a moment passed before the next *tring, tring*.

He said nothing, and I thought his silence meant he was plotting his revenge. If in the beginning he seemed pensive, and was incapable of making love, the time came when he wasn't so easygoing about hearing young and old alike uttering the alias I used in the ad—Katia—which sounded kind of Russian or Polish, as if I were a languid blonde with a beret and the face of someone in one of those plays where the good-looking girl can no longer bear the burden of her existence. [*That felt like an anachronism: for me, Katia was one of those Russian or Polish girls in customer-service departments.*] Before Fabio came along, I'd had to confront my unlikely "Katia" look on a daily basis, a dubious mirror that cracked every time they spoke my real name: Susana, Susana, Susana. I used to think Fabio ended up hearing those old and young men, those women, as if they were flies on the oilcloth during an after-dinner chat on a summer's evening. He'd raise his head, in confirmation of some tenuous life form, and then go on with whatever he had in hand, usually me, or the magazines he brought along to kill a weirdly alive time. I was incapable of putting my finger on exactly what had changed in the way he looked at me. And it was no use trying to make him participate in something that would relieve the monotony of the attic. But his cheekbones had become sharper, and there was something impenetrable in his gaze that hadn't been there before. It felt as though there was a judgment shining in his orange-flecked green eyes that made me yearn for that song about a laughing gnome. I couldn't remember who sung it, but did know the words. [*I believe she was referring to a David Bowie song I used to listen to as well, but in my case, I can't remember the lyrics.*] The gnome used to chuckle and cheer with the human friend whose side he never left. Although I couldn't put Fabio in my pocket, he was there like my court jester, entertaining me in a way my medication prevented me from appreciating. He was that broken modernist tile on an old floor you can't find a replacement for, which you stub your toe on whenever you've put too much milk in your coffee; one day, you're barefoot, and it's not a matter of the hot, creamy liquid falling through the air to land on your foot, it's that you've cut your toe and can't walk. I couldn't walk. That happened in July. We'd reverted to daylight savings that year, there were long days again, and it was a real pleasure to go to La Almudena cathedral to watch the light fade with those flitting threads of cloud over Casa del Campo Park, Paseo Extremadura, and Somosaguas. The sky was low, as if trying to say something to the bits of urban landscape whose hysterical brick bodies poked up between the weeds and the distance. Having Fabio there beside me, not showing the least emotion, spoiled my ecstasy. One day I asked him to start coming later. "How about ten o'clock?" I was free to go to my meetings at the Huertas bar again, but I had no takers in those first days. I didn't have the courage to make the opening move, so I went instead to El Viaducto in La Latina and watched the twilight colors from the bridge, with the bats flitting around the streetlights. And that's what I did all through June. They hadn't installed the suicide barriers then, and people used to jump off. In spite of the traffic, the way the organs of the dead person exploded with the sound of a breaking yogurt carton felt very close to my ears. The threads of blood trickled along Calle Segovia; they were like liquid claw marks. The weird zigzagging disposition of the limbs allowed you to hypothesize on the number of broken bones; half of the body, in its static dance, was by then a disgusting fusion-cuisine mass of tissue and asphalt. Occasionally you could see the inside of the cranium, the cluster of brains, the shining sweetbreads. [*I frowned. For some time my preliminary objection had been nagging at me: Why exaggerate something I could check? And why couldn't I accept she did whatever she liked with the story of her life, that she reinvented herself whatever way she felt sounded best?*] When August came, and it was as if there was no one in the city— people used to go on holiday en masse, and you could hear a leaf drop three streets away—I got tired of watching the suicides, and arranged to meet with one of the voices, the most attractive one: I'd gotten more particular since Fabio. Just anybody wasn't good enough. I didn't even need them to carry out my request. I arrived at the bar—the walls were by then bright blue instead of green—and a graying, fiftyish man was waiting at my usual table, reading the newspaper. I'd just turned twenty-seven, and though I never worried about age, I judged him too old. The size of his body should have made him more desirable than Fabio, but it didn't. I sat down; something had changed, my senses weren't as dulled by the medication. I'd become accustomed to the chemicals by then, and my metabolism made me like someone who, after three months sleeping in the open air on an ice sheet, had managed to build an igloo. The table was the snow over which I now slid with the elegance of a hare. I rested my elbows on it, and gave the man a flirtatious look; I was as ugly as ever, but I guess my face was no longer the reflection of chaotic mental processes, because he looked at me with a degree of pleasure, without a trace of the shock they used to observe me with before.

"Pleased to meet you," he said.

"My name's Susana, not Katia," I replied.

"All the girls lie about their names. I'm Paco."

We shook hands as formally as if we were about to have a work meeting.

"I like your name."

"I like yours too. More than Katia. That made me think you were some kind of third-party agency."

"I'm not an agency."

"Right. What do you do?"

"Just now, nothing. I'm taking a year out."

"That's nice. I'm a nursing assistant. Have you been doing this dating thing for long?"

"A year, on and off. I always have ads posted. You?"

"I've only been calling numbers for two weeks. You didn't specify what you wanted in your advertisement."

"I'm not really sure what I want."

"That makes me think we won't be seeing each other again."

"You're probably right," I responded. "I've got a boyfriend."

"And do you cheat on him often?"

"I've never cheated on him. What are you looking for?"

"A stable relationship. But if something else comes along, I won't let the opportunity pass."

"I'm glad you're not sentimental. Where do you work?"

"At the Fundación Jiménez Díaz. I'm divorced, with three children. I have a good relationship with my ex."

"Great," I replied.

I felt an urge to be honest with him, and eventually said, "I'm not exactly certain I've got a boyfriend."

I noticed a balloon working its way free and rising under the pressure of its compressed air. Paco gave me a wary look, so I qualified:

"What I mean is I've been with someone for a few months, but haven't decided if I want to stay with him yet."

Has it ever occurred to you that naming what's happening to you is a betrayal, but that, years afterward, you can talk about the past as if it were inside a jam jar with all its ingredients listed? I thought some kind of dignity that had to be maintained out of respect for the facts was demanding I should politely stand up and say goodbye to Paco. If I did it immediately, I felt my words would lose their effect. Paco would be an illusion. Nevertheless, I sat there waiting for him to ask me more questions so I could go on manipulating the story. I wanted him to save me from guilt. He didn't save me from anything. Paco was a practical man, and he said, "Talking through a problem from every angle has never solved anything. Whatever you do, you should feel good about it."

Self-help wasn't yet in vogue then, and he sounded to me like a priest going back on what he's said. Before I go on about Paco, I want you to note down that phrase. Have you got paper? I don't want to have to get my laptop right now. [*We kept notepaper and a pen in the chest of drawers, but I took out my cell phone and struggled with the touch-screen keyboard. The phrase Susana wanted me to write down made no sense.*] I don't use notebooks any longer. Do you? I just buy one from time to time for sketching. But, let's see: I was at the bar with Paco, and the truth is I was really feeling at ease, but with no idea what to do next. I remember Paco smiling at me, waiting for me to decide on the tone of our meeting. You could tell he was good-natured. We could even have parted then like two people satisfied with having fulfilled our desires, because the starting line of hope was still in non-painful regions. I'm much worse now than I was in those months after the loss of my mental health. Because I was so empty, I made room for anything, and I was like a coat of curiosity on a hanger, a coat that was gradually being filled, like a tower of clothes, until I became greedy again.

"I like you," Paco said, and blushed from the neck up.

I pretended I hadn't noticed, and soon his face was bronzed again in a way that reminded me of *dulce de leche*. As if he was suppurating sugar. I looked at him carefully. What had seemed like a dull speck of sweetness was in fact dry skin beneath his five o'clock shadow. I felt slightly nauseous.

"I'm not feeling too good," I said.

Paco went to the bathroom to dampen a white hand-kerchief embroidered with his initials. He pressed it to my wrists: the gesture seemed to me old fashioned and wrong. Yet I didn't stop him. I sat with my arms stretched out on the table, pretending to feel faint, trying to check if the hand-kerchief had been used. Cotton handkerchiefs make me cringe. [*I recalled a blind date with a university professor who had contacted me through Facebook; he was a friend of a friend, and his comments seemed intelligent. I'd just finished a relation-ship, and was looking for things to do, not really interested in meeting anyone, but with that dim consciousness of "You have to get out, you have to meet people, there are other fish in the sea," and other popular syntactic strings, only partially applicable, like any law, like statistics. I'd always trusted in time and the will-power I was able to find in solitude; I mean, I agreed to meet the professor because of other people's concern, not because I had any desire to go fishing. We went to a restaurant that served designer food. The professor was boring; he was no different from the man Susana was telling me about, a little empathy, but he'd started explaining his projects, taking it for granted I'd be interested in his stories as long as they were exhaustive. His voice was pleas-ant, his anecdotes well focused, and they more than fulfilled their initial function: giving me a detailed, theoretically entertaining report of his work, not omitting all the hours he'd spent alone during the last week or month, because his words oozed a need to recount what had been for so long only a conversation with him-self. There was no desire to dazzle, or to present himself as some-thing he wasn't, or to feign ingenuousness. But he was a bit of a disappointment. His block narrative left no room for dialogue. Other fish in the sea. I felt I truly understood the meaning of that*

maxim because there were no other fish in sight: the saying sud-
denly felt powerful precisely because of my disillusion, in which
I would discover a new faith. We have no option but to place
convenient levels of faith in general statements. And what was
convenient for me was to tear at my flesh. I didn't want the pain,
but there was no way to avoid it. Marinated salmon, an escarole
salad that looked like green coral or those little trees of moss I used
to pull from saffron milk cap mushrooms when I treated myself
to them. That evening we also treated ourselves to one of the va-
riety of mushrooms in season: amanita ponderosa, *resembling*
rocky outcrops or clouds coated in mud. But the brown wasn't
mud; it was a fine skin over parallel strings of veins—live flesh
of the earth. I remember the professor taking out a white cotton
handkerchief to blow his nose, a handkerchief similar to the one
my grandmother used to keep in her sleeve, and that was the last
straw. What I felt wasn't disgust, or not a bodily disgust, but a
disgust of the image. I am capable of that level of superficiality:
I don't like men who use cotton handkerchiefs. That certainty be-
gan to slide toward the precarious zone of generalities I thought
all the more frivolous for being manipulative. I don't like men
who use cotton handkerchiefs is a stupid thing to say, and I was
disconcerted to have gotten stuck on the least eloquent of phrases
instead of going one step further and saying: too professorial, or
too organized, or our life plans don't match (more lies). Yes, I was
exaggerating, but my heart was more than cold, and I guess his
was too. It was an impasse.] I stayed there for a while with my
arms tensed on the tabletop, allowing Paco to feel like the
typical urban hero, appearing from nowhere to help the girl
who's fainted because of some subtle, neurotic fear. I didn't
really mind that image, and I don't think Paco did either; I

mean, nothing was at stake for either of us, except a tepid layer of courtesy and padding, the stage props within which I discovered myself to be a person who didn't need pills. What a relief!

"I'm much better now, thanks," I said, withdrawing my arm.

Paco rose tactfully from his chair and I followed his example. We went fifty-fifty on the check, and the kind gentleman gave me his phone number, telling me to call if I came to a decision.

"I might not be at that number by then. You know how these things are..." he added.

It was the perfect, classic ending. I went back to the attic, and Fabio arrived almost immediately. He didn't ask me where I'd been, even though his sense of smell must have registered the range of odors from the bar: reheated croissants, toasted sandwiches, the toasted sandwich bread, cigarettes. Nowadays no one smokes with that bizarre determination to be cloaked in a hard, noisy, stale, stuffy atmosphere. We got down to our daily ritual; afterward, he pressed the button on the answering machine and turned up the volume to hear the recorded voices. The last one was Paco's.

"Susana," he said, "It was lovely to spend the evening with you. Whatever you do about that boyfriend of yours, remember I'm here for anything you want."

I thought over those words, as if they contained something more than pleasant simplicity. Then I looked at Fabio, his face now turned to the wall, and as flat as the wall in its embarrassment at his sadness.

"Sorry," I said.

I pulled out the telephone cord and we ate in silence, because I didn't have the courage to ask him to tell me about his work at the NIC, to give me an update on his olfactory investigations. It had also been one of his days for tests at the research center. Having done an in-depth analysis of the structure of his nose, they were now studying his brain. They did CAT scans to check which areas were activated by smells; only strong ones produced clear enough changes in the neurons. The reaction of Fabio's brain to the ink on newsprint or documents was extremely subtle, and the machines weren't very precise. I missed that everyday routine, even if I did think it fair to have to manage without it. I couldn't tell him anything either; whatever I said would be just an attempt to soften my betrayal. We went to bed; Fabio made love to me. He wanted me to look him in the eyes. Halfway through he put my legs over his shoulders, those puny shoulders that could scarcely move under the weight of my mammoth thighs. He wanted me to see how his body had to strain not to give way. I closed my eyes, but he said, "Look at me. I'm not going to come if you won't look at me. Look me in the eye."

It was pure morbid curiosity for what would come: hatred, and the taste of turpentine beneath the tongue. When it was finished, we didn't even speak, and the bed became a frontier whose barbed wire it was best not to prowl along. Fabio moved right up against the wall, and I lay on the other extreme of the mattress, with part of my body hanging over, noting how the cold rose up from the floor. There were a couple of feet between us; when nocturnal movements made our legs brush against each other, we woke in disgust, and then increased the distance again. We were like two utility poles with the cables cut.

The next day, I made an appointment with another of the voices, this time a woman. I needed to quench my thirst for female friends. For two hours, we told each other our troubles, and I was content. Fabio arrived at the apartment at ten and pressed play; that day I had the impression there were no gaps between one voice and the next, as if they were taking turns to speak during one continuous call. Toward the end, the voices merged in what could have been called a Singles Chorus, and I had a sudden anxiety attack, similar to the ones I suffered in the days before my psychosis. I had to sit down; fear was snaking around, and I think Fabio realized it, because a look of pity appeared on his face. For a moment he didn't seem to remember who we were, and when his features turned hard again, I wanted to ask him to please look at me for a few moments more as if I wasn't me, but anyone about to jump off El Viaducto, one of those suicides like a grape falling from a vine that make you think real maturity is the sort that leaves you at the doors of death, and that the people who jumped weren't desperate; they had arrived at their end, and were just being practical.

I slept badly. Despite having disconnected the phone, I kept waking throughout the night with the sensation a crowd of people was moving around the attic, a crowd that had gotten in through the telephone. That's how the phone looked to me: small, but with a door the size of a person on one of its sides. At times I thought they weren't human, they were the spirits of other, earlier nights that had sneaked into my room through the voices and the red light of the answering machine that emitted its harsh throb in the darkness. This hypothesis wasn't viable during my brief spells of half sleep, because there was no red light, just the clear light of day, and the noise of the crowd. I could have sworn I didn't sleep the whole night, but when I opened my eyes, I was surprised by the silence, the metallic blue dawn in the window, and Fabio's small body without a sign of life. I put the mirror of my compact to his lips, because I was afraid he'd died. The glass misted with his microscopic breath. It wasn't the first time I'd done that; on other mornings, when I couldn't sleep and saw his back so still—cold and still, as if rest froze him—I'd run for my makeup bag. Just putting my hand to his lips wasn't enough. On a couple of occasions, I'd woken him in terror; after three minutes Fabio's skin would regain color, and his rib cage would move in the rhythm of regular human respiration. [*I allowed myself to be carried along by the narrative. I've always liked stories of the living dead, and Ouija board sessions. I wondered if that was my way of listening: only believing what I endorsed.*] I had the urge to tell him that perhaps the keenness of his sense of smell had something to do with that nocturnal plunge into some region where air was hardly necessary, but that would have given away the weird, shameful effect his inert body had on me, and Fabio had already had more than enough of the spectacle of my non-love. Without warning, I suddenly felt infinite compassion for him, for his circus-performer dwarf flesh. And then, what good would it do him to know that, on many nights, I woke to find him like a corpse? At the same time, I wanted to stand in front of those people who were investigating him and ask how they thought simple machines could measure Fabio's ability to skirt death. If the machines reached that region of the underworld, they would shatter, or maybe register absurd, terrifying images the researchers would reject, but which you could use to write poetry. Could Fabio in fact be one of the ghosts from my answering machine? I'm not certain now what I'm telling you, but at the time I never allowed myself to doubt those purely intuitive sensations that explained things without touching any of the borders of reason.

And then suddenly it was winter. If I work it out carefully, there was no way winter had come around so soon, but it was cold, the mornings were misty, with those January and February mists of the Castilian plains, and the bars of the electric heater emitting their orange warmth, and from my attic overlooking Calle San Ginés you couldn't see any bare trees, but their loneliness came to me from the parks, as if trees had telepathic powers. That was the first time I heard them, and from that moment, in some way I can't quite explain, I've never stopped hearing them. I could still put it down to the effects of my medication then, but not now. For me, the present is eternity; when my stomach aches, I think I'm going to have to go around hunched over forever, and the situation with my tiny Fabio felt eternal for the same reason.

I like to tell the ending this way, though it's not completely true: one day, Fabio disappeared. For weeks, I tried to sort out what I'd learned with him. Why I'd used our relationship. I stopped taking my pills, got a job as a waitress at night, and started going to college in the afternoons. I felt vulnerable, but in a sane rather than pathological way. I was in that state when I met the engineer. Look, the only man I had during my mad period was Fabio, so there was no way I wasn't going to appreciate the engineer, even if he was a son of a bitch. The engineer was tall, and his bones weren't about to crumble. And what's more, I had doubts about the accuracy of my memory of what I'd been through, because when I stopped taking the medication, my nervous system went back to a different perception of things. [*Why had she put off explaining herself for so long? Had she been trying to keep me on tenterhooks? I felt slightly disappointed.*] As must be clear from what I've just told you, I can't go to any therapist or psychiatrist with this story of a dwarf with an extraordinary sense of smell without them telling me I had, throughout that whole period, in some toned-down way, been hallucinating, or that there had been something so painful and censurable in what I'd actually done that I exchanged it for an imaginary story. It doesn't bother me. When someone looks at me reproachfully, I always think of the smell of coffee-flavored candy on the breath of the priest at my high school. Don José always used to have a bulge in his cheek because, we supposed, he'd stuffed in four cream toffees to suck during the hours we children told him our little droplets of sin: I pulled my sister's hair; I grabbed her around the throat, squeezed hard, she went red, and I almost killed her; I cheated on my exams, I'd promised never to do it again but…how do I know if God really exists? I used to summon him up after the hilarious catechesis: If you really exist, make the traffic signal turn green when I want to cross the street. God doesn't manifest himself just because you want him to, the nun would tell me. Didn't you do things like that? [*I have no memory of having worried about the existence of God, and I told her so. That was the second time I'd spoken.*] I'm agnostic these days, but as a child I became an atheist. A devout atheist. I can only use hackneyed religious references to describe what I intended to get from a revelation that would occur in the most ordinary of situations, in the rupture of a mechanism only I witnessed. Of course, I didn't actually expect the traffic signal to turn green three seconds after it had turned red; God producing such a blatant short circuit wasn't any part of my desire, because it would have meant he didn't appreciate my intelligence. What I expected were small slips in reality no one else could see. Maybe you think it was just vanity, a silly desire to be chosen by God as the person he would manifest himself to, but it wasn't like that. What I was searching for was that door the saints and mystics talk about: seeing God reveal himself in everything. To see him, not with the eyes, because I knew no light was going to pass through the wall, but through strange conjunctions, through artistic rather than religious epiphanies. Nevertheless, on those spring afternoons when I was making my way to the crosswalk after my religious instruction class, all I saw was the sidewalk without a single crack, so solid beneath my feet, and the sturdy trunks of the plane trees with their warm leaves etched against the sky, and the curb with its sash of cars. A sense of supreme impenetrability would be emanating from the traffic signal at the end of the street whose casing, instead of being empty, made you think of more metal, of tons of metal, so heavy it frightened off any phenomenon except its own stubborn material. Nothing happened, just that one-way street, trees on one side, shops and doorways on the other, the exhaust fumes from cars forming short-lived strips at ground level. One day, when the traffic signal was yellow, an old woman was knocked down. Her wig fell at my feet with shop-window composure: the perfect chignon, not a single hair out of place. Her body seemed as heavy as the traffic signal. It had that same composition without the cracks in which I'd vainly hoped the divine would present itself. That's why I say I was an atheist, because I faithfully believed in the simple presence of things, and in their even more simple disappearance. I was left with a sense of remorse for not having helped the old lady. I ran away as if my life depended on it—as if death was going to stab me. The result of a conversion to atheism is that you suddenly believe in death. You believe in death more than in anything else. [*There must have been something equivocal in one of my gestures or facial expressions, judging by the silence that fell when Susana pronounced the word "death"; her body seemed to tense slightly, and I thought that, in some place my medication prevented me from reaching, fluttered a question with my name on it. Susana, however, went on.*]

PART TWO

A WORKING WOMAN

My financial situation wasn't good. I'd had to exchange my apartment in Plaza Tirso for another in Aluche, at the top of a hill where the buildings were set amid a wasteland of sites awaiting development. They told me it was the hill from which Antonio López García painted one of his realistic cityscapes, but the only thing I found during my internaut search was a painting of Vallecas and another entitled *South Madrid* that didn't match what I could see from the window. It was, nevertheless, similar, especially when the steamy, ashen cloud rose from the asphalt and exhaust pipes, and mingled with the summer sunlight, so every time I went to the roof I was convinced it was the exact spot from which the panorama of the south of Madrid stretched out in the painting.

I worked in the living room, facing the sea of redbrick buildings, and above the wasteland, where pale yellow hedge mustard grew in clumps of earth. Every Monday I'd go to the seventh floor of the publishing house to hand in my work. In the early days, when I was based in the office, I thought it would be a kind of liberation to work on the documents I was proofreading from home, because I detested having to cross the city. I had to travel to Quinta de los Molinos, with two changes and a brief wait on Avenida de América, where the dust particles in the air seemed to stick in the folds in my clothing. The conversations with Felipe and Asun by the coffee machine were no compensation for the boredom of spending eight hours poring over galleys in a room with no windows and a low plaster ceiling.

When independent contractors turned up as if they were inside an air bubble, I couldn't help feeling jealous, and I used to imagine that, after dropping off their piles of paper, they would wander aimlessly around Parque Quinta, along the strange avenues of almond and olive trees coated in frost in winter, or allow themselves the luxury of doing what I would have liked to do every morning of my working life before entering the office: crossing the park and getting lost among the factories that sprouted up here and there, as though sprinkled in some kind of Chinese dish of dilapidated residential buildings. I used to go out for a walk sometimes too, but I'd already be tired, so it wasn't the same. Before losing my full employee status, I'd considered the possibility of asking my bosses if I could work from home a couple of days a week. By the time they announced they were going to convert me into a contractor, my salary had already been cut, and I was having problems making it through to the end of the month.

I'd asked the people at the Public Housing

Association to broaden their search for a single person's whatever-they-could-manage to outlying neighborhoods. I was about to resign myself to a room in a shared apartment when they called with an offer to show me the place in Aluche. The rent was €440, the limit of what I was willing to pay, but also the bottom limit of what I might be able to find, barring some miracle of the pre-1985 rental laws. I'd already shifted my search toward the south of the city, and one rainy afternoon included in its sweep Delicias as far as the M-30 beltway. The day I said yes to the Association, I crossed that beltway by one of those ugly iron bridges with long stretches of unnecessary stairs, and made my way along Usera and then Carabanchel without— for the first time in four months—stopping to jot down the telephone numbers on FOR RENT signs. On General Ricardos, I boarded a bus and alighted at a temporary stop on a street of modest two-story houses that had somehow avoided demolition.

Becoming an independent contractor had been the first step. Then they started getting behind with my paychecks, only making them promptly when I complained. They used to say this courtesy—meeting their obligations—was a sign of how much they valued me. When winter came around, I hadn't been paid for two months, and I'd started, without much success, testing the waters at other publishing houses. I worked till late on galleys that left me without the slightest desire to read or go on looking at the screen, and then I'd need to get outside, walk and have a couple of beers. The winter they were late paying me was bitterly cold; there was ice everywhere that stuck to the surfaces of things in a way that refuted the laws of nature, as if a heavy early morning dew refused to disperse.

I had no desire to see that ice or to freeze, and given the fact that I was incapable of staying indoors, my walks began to change into a sort of race during which I initially managed not to look at anything. I'd just concentrate on my breathing, following the same line of thinking that, a year before, had led me to cross the M-30 and stroll along Carabanchel and Usera. For a month I went as far as Eugenia de Montijo, to a park from which I could observe the progress being made in demolishing the old prison, and I'd stand there looking at the stones for a long time, because the desolation was comforting. Then I'd return home on the metro, or on foot. When my need for flight grew stronger, I started taking buses. I didn't travel very far; among other things, the regular service stopped at eleven thirty. But the journey was long enough for me to begin composing a sort of mental itinerary that functioned as a very effective form of evasion. The Colonia San Ignacio de Loyola, General Fanjul, Carpetana, Plaza Elíptica, certain stretches of empty avenues that gave me the pleasant sensation of being somewhere else, Leganés in the distance when I decided to travel south to view the hills and the manic traffic on the highway.

I'd sometimes sit down on the bus, although I normally stood near the driver, which allowed me to eavesdrop on his or sometimes her conversations with the retirees who boarded the bus at that hour (I swear they were almost always retirees). For the duration of those journeys along streets I'd always remember clearly afterward, I used to think up solutions to my financial worries, like renting out the former dressing room in the apartment; however, I soon realized I didn't want anyone else in my home and, what's more, I'd slipped into a kind of paradoxical sense of déjà vu, because all my master's degrees, and the time I'd spent abroad, now seemed like a negation in advance of what was happening to me. In other words, in a roundabout way, I'd been preparing myself for something like this. That was no consolation or justification, yet it did permit me to gloat over the strangeness that always seems to tinge a slightly stupid poetic sense of things, and from there I'd come up with the idea that the situation was just a type of hiatus. Some evenings I returned to an old routine, from the time I shared a duplex on Metropolitana and would go to watch the sunset and the encroaching dark from Alto de Extremadura. Nearby there were microbuses that circulated around the whole district, and one of the routes terminated on a hillside with a construction site, not so different from where I live now, which made me think I was predestined to reside in my new home. That microfiction served as a means of addressing the whole affair.

SHORT STORY PUBLISHED IN A DEFUNCT SPANISH NEWSPAPER

1

It was a November morning. The cars were all covered in a fine coating of snow that contrasted with the black of the sidewalk. I was constantly wiping the windowpanes in a compulsive desire for the outside world to penetrate the apartment just as it presented itself to me through the glass: an enormous open sky. However, what I was on the point of receiving was—or so I'd imagined—small and trivial, and about to occupy one of the bedrooms. I'd had the impression I was living with someone else from the moment Germán recommended her to me, and I'd behaved as if the spare room was already inhabited; the small spare room whose dirt-smudged walls I'd neither painted nor wiped down, at the window of which I used to smoke. I'd tidied it in advance, but without making much of an effort. And I'd stopped going in there for cigarette breaks. Nevertheless, that morning I spent quite a while standing by that cold window, looking into the distance without knowing what to ask of it. Perhaps I was afraid.

It was twelve thirty when she arrived. She wasn't, as I'd hoped, short and plump like a Hispanic mother, but the Nordic type: tall, blond, horsey, with a complexion the color of something like raw silk. She was squeezed into a brown coat that came down to her ankles, and had a showy beige scarf around her neck. On her head was a green hat, with a swirl on one side like a flower. Weighed down by so much wool, she could hardly move, and her cheeks briefly glowed with two perfect, rosy circles. She was a bit ridiculous, particularly due to something that seemed to have its source in her nose, which, from the instant she crossed the threshold, appeared unpleasantly on the alert for any smell, the nostrils flared and quivering. It was such an eloquent gesture that, if I hadn't previously committed myself, I would never have considered accepting her as a roommate, and nor would she have taken the tiny room. After she'd removed her coat, the hat, and several cardigans, settled her horrendous heavy-rimmed glasses, and looked at me with eyes trembling in time to her rat's nose, she huffed and said, "My name's Susana, though I suppose you already know that. I'd like to have spoken to you first, buuuut…"

Then she muttered something quickly, but I didn't catch what it was. I introduced myself, asked her a few questions about her journey (Germán had told me she was arriving from Utrecht, where she'd been living for seven years), and led her to the room.

"See you later," she said, shutting the door.

I made coffee and sat at the dining-room table, facing the balcony. The pattern of the ice on the pane (not on the edges, but in the center) was like a Dantesque spider thrown from the street and, as it melted, slowly spilled its guts, leaving a thread that made the forms ascending the hill look grainy. I could see through her pretense, which was also mine, since I was hoping Susana would find me attentive but not too attentive. When I'd had enough, I went to her room, knocked a couple of times, and opened the door. I found her sitting on the bed, her suitcases unopened, with tears in her eyes. I asked if I could do anything, she said no. After a while, she came out and left the rent on the chest of drawers in the living room. Then she walked to the door, went out into the street, and didn't come back for five days.

Her absence annoyed me. I'd been preparing myself for a modification in my routine since I'd agreed to Germán's proposition. I kept the place tidy, because I thought it was my duty to make a good impression, but Susana showed no signs of turning up again, and I went to bed grumbling to myself. What's more, I couldn't smoke my cigarettes while looking out on the street from the window; the room wasn't mine now, although it wasn't hers either. I went in there and observed all those unfamiliar objects. They were so predictable, they didn't even personalize the bedroom, and except for the neatly made bed and the wardrobe full of clothes, it looked like no one was ever going to sleep there, as if the room's only purpose was to store things that had overflowed from somewhere else, which left me in a state close to paranoia.

And during those five days of waiting, I also considered a more profound, undoubtedly more petty-minded question: Why was it that she'd disappeared, oozing independence through every pore, while I was stuck here with my ghosts?

It was a time of despair, and perhaps that explained my misgivings. Day after day, I got out of bed with a growing sense of anxiety that lasted well into the afternoon, when my apprehensions would vanish without anything having happened to justify the change. I'd lie on the bed and welcome sleep as a blessed relief. In addition to the extra money it brought in, the decision to rent the room involved making an effort to shake off my depressive inertia, but my insignificant-girl desire sprung directly from that inertia. At heart I didn't want anyone else there to interrupt the constant digression from myself to myself, the perpetual pacing from one room to another, the unbearably limited territory that stretched from the front door to the living room, the living room to my bedroom, the kitchen, the bathroom.

The day she finally reappeared, she was wearing the same clothes as when she left. When she took off her coat, I noticed some round stains on her sweater, glistening like fresh grease. She sat on the sofa and started speaking, taking for granted I had some idea what she'd been doing. She referred to an argument with the receptionist at a diet and nutrition center, and spoke about the lobbies of certain hotels. Then she mentioned salaries and a personality test, and it dawned on me she'd been looking for work. She hadn't, she told me, had a moment to spare, she was getting home in the early hours, going straight to bed, and getting up again at seven. "Right," I said. It was Susana who put an end to the conversation, but not before offering—because I asked her—a few brief, dry facts about her life: she was born in Madrid, had grown up in Chamberí, and seven years before had gone to live in Utrecht with her Dutch boyfriend, whom she'd met in the Education Department at the university here. He'd been on an Erasmus scholarship.

That same afternoon the changes began in my unhappy apartment. First she moved everything around in the kitchen, since she thought my organization was haphazard. By nightfall, cutlery, pans, plates, and glasses were arranged in such a way that they seemed to have been made to occupy a specific space. Of course, I resolved not to respect this new obsessive arrangement. The next day, in the early evening—my roommate had started working at a call center that morning—a messenger turned up with five moving boxes from Utrecht, and was greeted by a whoop of excitement—"My things!"—and clapping, while I stood by in horror: it was obvious all that stuff wouldn't fit in her room, and my small living room was going to be invaded. Which is exactly what happened. Over the next few days, the shelves were filled with books, leaves (they must have been from trees that grew in Canada or Japan, or some other place where those odd, unfading colors were common), cameras (she had nine), almanacs, and absurd objects of dubious utility. And everything placed any old how. In the same way that the picture Germán had painted of her didn't match what Susana turned out to be (he'd insisted she was an ordinary, obliging sort of person), the classificatory zeal she had displayed in the kitchen had nothing to do with the chaos of books, vials of colored salt, rubber dolls, sheet music, lighters, toy cars, Swatch wristwatches, Talavera pottery… I judged there must be an inherent lack of coherence in someone possessing such a wide array of different things, as if the person's tastes had yet to gel, and she'd decided to hoard stuff in the meantime. On the other hand, during those first days her room went from bland impersonality to what I believed to be a reflection of its inhabitant: candles shedding a very weak light, cups with flower designs, piles of clothes on the bed, and the horror vacui threatening to cover every single inch of wall in figures cut compulsively from magazines I suspected Susana must have taken from bars. Those magazines had lain discreetly by the bed on the days my roommate had disappeared from the scene, and I'd scarcely noticed them. One night I offered her a beer, and she told me the figures she chose were never actors or anything that could be counted as famous, since the worthy task of mythologizing didn't interest her. I examined the clippings; it has to be said she had an amazing talent for capturing secondary, underlying motifs that, seen in isolation, were not dissimilar to scenes in a Hieronymus Bosch, or a print from an Ivan Zulueta coloring book. She asked me if she could make a contribution to the decor of the apartment. I said she could. The next day, in a manner at once wary and menacing, she began to paste together tiny clippings—no larger than two inches in size—that would form a motif for the living room. In the kitchen, she arranged foodstuffs a la Arcimboldo; over the sofa, two statuesque women who reminded me of stuffed Persian cats; in the bathroom, bathtubs filled with bubbles. While I found them startling at first sight, the truth is that those figures did away with my tendency toward minimalism, which, in an apartment in Aluche with walls covered in textured paint, and furnishings from the era of my landlady's mother, didn't exactly give a Zen feel; it was disgusting.

Her miniscule clippings didn't bother me. But what did disturb me, particularly because I spent most of the day working in the dining room, were the shelves crammed with books and other items. Given that I was the person whose name was on the lease, why didn't it occur to me to set clear limits, such as respecting the way my stuff was arranged, or that her things belonged in her own room? I don't know why I didn't. I believe I convinced myself at the time that I had no right to such a prerogative. Susana had paid for her new home. And what's more, by not having set out rules from the start, I'd conceded the whole space.

We had conversations from time to time, although it would be more accurate to call them monologues, with her as the speaker. They were always on topics that bored me: the differences in the customs of Spain and Holland, recipes, exhaustive descriptions of movies or TV series. All this accompanied by complaints. If she told me she'd just seen a documentary at the indie theater, she'd heap insults on the member of the audience who had coughed, as if one caught a cold with the sole intention of annoying other people in movie theaters. She was completely obsessed with cultural matters, even though she wasn't really a cultured person, but then there were forbidden areas, like her job. The refusal to talk about her work was in notable contrast to the wealth of detail she had added when informing me how she'd obtained it. "I prefer not to waste my breath on that," she said. It didn't take me long to omit the "How was your day?" when she arrived home at five thirty.

All that didn't surprise me as much as the fact that, when we got to personal matters, the only things she mentioned had to do with her time in Utrecht, and her boyfriend, Janssen, whom she'd left behind there. Susana never talked about her family, and didn't seem to have ever lived in any neighborhood. I tried approaching her past from less compromised regions, and was rewarded with the same silence, as if I hadn't spoken. When I overheard her talking with her *friends* on the telephone, I realized there was no real friendship in the conversations, no intimacy between herself and the people with whom she spoke—just as she did with me—about movies, concerts, or exhibitions. It was as if they were new friends, or merely acquaintances.

And, to my displeasure, I also began coming across her outside the apartment: on my Saturday trip to the supermarket; when I occasionally went to the movies or met someone for dinner. I went out very little then, and it seemed strange that we should meet when I did. A couple of friends who lived nearby, and who came to dinner one Sunday, also started to run into her and, while they liked her, they too noticed something dark, an excess that made her a recurrent topic of conversation. One day, I had the feeling she was following me. I was walking to Café Barbieri when, turning into Argumosa, I bumped into Susana, who quickly turned and started talking to a person whose face I couldn't see. I watched her out of the corner of my eye, and had the impression it wasn't possible she knew that person, but she didn't continue on her way, and, once inside the café, I thought I glimpsed her in the mirror, lurking in the doorway. Susana informed me she spent certain evenings rediscovering (that was the word she used) the city. She had no problem with striking up conversations with strangers. According to her, she didn't often waste money in bars, and having an avid curiosity, had found places—usually rundown or alternative—where she could spend hours without attracting attention at some form of cultural event. From time to time she'd tell me whom she'd met, and didn't spare any details. She seemed to be looking for an equal, or a home. Her nose—that subtle barometer of smells that registered what only a canine or some other animal was capable of appreciating—would cease its spasmodic twitching in the evening when she got back from work to find me making coffee. I couldn't not invite her to share, and ended up using the large coffee pot. In my case, the result was drinking three cups instead of one. Taking cover behind my invitation, I'd watch her put her coat on a hanger in the hall, go to the bathroom to wash her hands, and then take a seat. She always arrived with a baguette, from which she pulled pieces to soak in the black liquid, never going to her room until it was all consumed. Those coffees began to bring us closer. As there was no overt admission that we were sharing time together, Susana sometimes didn't turn up, or I might be out. Not taking it for granted we would meet up made me more relaxed. I went on enjoying my three cups even when my roommate wasn't present, since I'd become addicted to the stimulation caused not by imbibing a lot of coffee throughout the day, but by chain-drinking. Another pleasure was added to this, tobacco: I sometimes smoked a whole pack in a few hours. The overdose of caffeine and nicotine didn't help my growing state of mental instability, and some nights, to counteract my nerves, I'd put on an oversized tracksuit and go running for an hour.

2

Whenever I came across the guys from the truck, I'd wrap my coat around myself so they wouldn't shout abuse at me. In the past I'd always seen them downtown, after midnight. I hadn't realized they had started carrying out their activities on the outskirts of the city, although it was logical they would, since the traffic dies down earlier, and there's no police presence these days. They would have been between fourteen and sixteen when I was twenty, and ran into them for the first time. They threw a piece of a box studded with staples at me, and it scraped my face before landing in one of the flowerbeds around the Neptune fountain. Then they laughed. They were just a small group of kids, mostly Romanies, who collected boxes, and shouted at any young woman they came across. They also ran from the local police, and the garbage trucks, which were competition; and perhaps from someone whose forehead they'd smashed with a piece of metal thrown from the truck. I once saw them breaking a car window with a heavy drawer. The glass made a sound like pebbles falling down a slope; their laughter froze. In a sense it was as if they had some kind of dark motor inside their vehicle (the sort of truck you might expect to disgorge a sheep or some other rural element). I didn't run into them often after that first occasion, and they never threw anything at me again. What they did was shout, whistle, jubilantly launch some piece of unmitigated abuse, and then vanish onto a side street. Their ubiquity reminded me of the man with white hair, a crazy we've all seen sometime or other in free movie screenings, or standing in the shade of a tree on Pintor Rosales, rocking his Chinese girlfriend's wheelchair. During the time I had my fixed-term contracts and an apartment downtown, I didn't see them, because I was no longer the night owl I'd been in college. I only ever went to the local bar, and on weekends rarely ventured more than a few steps further to the left or right, to Lavapiés or La Latina, streets which were too narrow to escape onto. It was only since I'd started taking walks again that they had reappeared. They were older now, and didn't shout at me. Even so, I felt exactly the same uneasiness; I was afraid they would throw the edge of some stapled box at me again. In anticipation of the blow, I'd shut my eyes, which stopped me from getting a closer look at them. The truck moved away, leaving a trail of cardboard scraps, and the smells of burned grass and stripped furniture. They were scarcely shadows peeking out from between the sheet metal. Age had cloaked them in a discretion I liked, if only at a distance.

3

When Susana moved into the apartment, I hadn't been paid
for a few months, and my attempts to find a place in some
other publishing house had come to nothing. My roommate
was paid punctually for her work at the call center, and didn't
have to give it a second thought after five, while I would
be battling with galleys until eight, and constantly waiting
to be paid. Some nights I'd slave away on proofs until ten
or eleven, not that I spent all that time hunting for errors.
What I was doing, with increasing frequency and without
the least benefit, was surfing the Internet. I'd visit the home
page of *El País* twenty times, look at the blogs I followed,
check out Facebook. It was a vicious circle, because the next
page of the galleys always held some unavoidable search,
infinitely duller than rereading the same newspaper head-
line: checking, for example, if the accent on *chérie* was acute
or grave. University professors, essayists, and even some fiction writers were used to having their dirty work done for

them, and the editor would decide this was the task of the independent contractor, who had no one making a note of her working hours, not even herself. I began wishing Susana would always turn up for our tacit five o'clock date, because after that long coffee break, I had the discipline not to waste any more time on the Internet. This new rhythm was only broken when, after a month and a half, Janssen, Susana's Dutch boyfriend, turned up. He stayed for a week, and my conversations with him were limited to the time it took him to eat a breakfast of Litoral canned beans in sauce. They argued on a daily basis—I couldn't help but overhear them—and when Janssen left, Susana spent the evenings on Skype, without even having coffee. While I was correcting proofs, I'd hear her speaking in English, a language that raised the pitch of her voice. My command of the language wasn't great, but even so, it was good enough to understand she was spending half the time pleading with him, and when I started feeling guilty (not so much for eavesdropping on her, as for the fact she knew I was listening), I decided to go to my own room. One evening she told me she'd split up with Janssen, so I put the large coffee pot back on the stove, and she sat on the sofa chewing on her bread. Then she made another pot, and snacked on cookies, while I smoked and ministered to her desolation. I was worried that she'd want to spend more time with me after the breakup to avoid feeling alone. My fears were unfounded, while she never missed a single coffee date, she didn't gabble on like crazy. One evening she asked, "You're Elisa Núñez, right?"

"Yes," I answered.

I didn't understand the question. Susana took a sheet of

crumpled newspaper from her backpack. Then I did get it.

"I spotted this at a friend's house," she clarified. "She's just come back from Italy, and all her things are in boxes. I was giving her a hand. She'd wrapped a cup in your text."

"Ah," was my only response.

I guessed that Susana had been searching my name on the Internet, and that made me uncomfortable.

"And you've published a novel too."

"That was a few years back, with a small publishing house, and I haven't written again seriously since then," I answered.

I wasn't lying. The crumpled text Susana was showing me was the last thing I'd written; and not because I'd wanted to: the Culture editor at the newspaper offered me three hundred euros. That text had been torture. I'd written it just before moving to Aluche, when I'd already seen the apartment and familiarized myself with the landscape, but before some of the things described there had begun to happen. I'm not superstitious; and anyway, everything I said in the text was in the air, and in some way existed in my desire, but I found the sensation of having written myself into those words distressing.

For a few days my roommate's voracious need to know directed the course of our conversations. Given her appetite for anything with a whiff of culture, it was perhaps inevitable that she would try to find a way to take an active role in that world. Her eyes sometimes expressed an exasperated tension, and reminded me of the presences around my bed during what was then a recurring dream that ended in a terrifying scene: a fade to black riveting my cervical vertebrae and screeches. I'd wake with the impression that a long nail had been scratching my flesh raw, and if it was the weekend, and I found Susana bent over her laptop in the living room (Monday to Friday she left the apartment before my alarm went off), it was like I'd discovered her hovering over my dream. To get my revenge for the sense of unease her spying caused me, I questioned her on a number of occasions about her childhood and life in Madrid before leaving for Utrecht, but as usual she warded off approaches with bizarre responses, or went to her room. The only mention of her past I managed to drag out of her was indirect. One day I rescued some of the books I used to read as a child from a high shelf. I asked her if she too had been a fan of the *Steamship* series. Susana took a graphic novel from her backpack and showed it to me, asking if I knew it. I shook my head, and she went on:

"The boy in this story lives in Detroit. His mother doesn't speak—just coughs and bangs doors. His brother doesn't speak either—he plays drums. His father is a radiologist, and practices boxing in the basement of the house. The boy suffers frequent chest problems. The father gives him X-ray treatment to cure his breathing difficulties, because that's what they did in those days. When he's eleven, the boy gets a lump in his throat, and someone suggests it's a tumor. The doctors examine him and think he has a sebaceous cyst, so they recommend surgery. The operation costs money, but his mother prefers to spend the father's annual raise on clothes. The operation is put off for three years. When he comes around from the anesthetic, he's missing one of his vocal cords, and the only sound he can make is 'aghhh.' Two weeks after returning home, he overhears his father saying that he has had cancer. Later still, his father confesses the X-ray sessions he'd prescribed were responsible for the malignancy. This is what I keep from my childhood."

I had no idea how to interpret that, or whether to respond with more graphic novels or family illnesses. I felt that, while asking her directly would somehow fling her into a very painful place, I was missing an opportunity to get to know something essential about her.

4

The Grupo Editorial Término had been at the top of a list on a form I'd filled out five years prior, giving my preferences for the practical element of a master's in publishing. The internship included the possibility of a contract, and a contract was the most basic aspiration of the eighty people who turned up every Friday and Saturday to be taught the trade. My publishing group, whose imprints were mentioned most frequently on the form, was responsible for the administration of the master's degree. After the internship, I was given three consecutive temporary contracts, and then came the crisis: the business had serious losses and there were pay cuts, with those of us on temporary contracts being converted to independents. Apart from a decrease in my earnings, this implied proofreading not only for my usual imprint, but also for the paperback collection, which covered all varieties of books, including first editions. Initially, I didn't complain or seek out solidarity. I wasn't even interested in knowing how many contracted employees had changed status in the other imprints. Nor did I keep in touch with any of my former colleagues. Our friendships—if they could have been called that—were constantly pierced by the sharp knife-edge of competition, of those fine, exhausting typographical characters, the ownership of which was always being evaluated.

"The boiler's broken down again," said Carmentxu when I turned up in her office.

"No kidding," I replied.

I went over to the radiator to check it was in fact cold. It was an awkward situation: the whole way there I'd been chewing over a question that had to be simple but barbed, and suddenly, faced with a comment absolutely unrelated to the rumors of layoffs I'd heard that morning—the motive for my visit—it felt impossible to lead the conversation in that direction. I did not, however, give in easily, and with ill-concealed brusqueness, said, "What's happening with my overdue pay?"

"I wanted to talk to you about that," replied Carmentxu. "We're going to release some of your payments. The ones for urgent books. And when the cash flow eases, we'll sort out the rest. It's our way of helping you out a little. They don't think it will take more than three months for things to get back to normal."

"Sure," I answered.

Out of sheer bullheadedness, I wanted to inquire about where this money was coming from, but I didn't. Carmentxu huffed uncomfortably; perhaps my agitation was unsettling her. I finally asked about the layoffs, and she gave me an exact replica of the rumor I'd already heard. I wasn't surprised she didn't know any more than I did.

"I'm feeling upbeat, because I'm still here, and that forces me to be optimistic, but anything could happen. It's been quite a few months now. I don't know if we're all going to end up in the shit, but sometimes I wish it would just happen. Want a coffee?"

"Tea, I think."

On that floor there was a machine dispensing hot, sugary liquid stimulants. With the impression I was scorching my vocal cords, I quickly gulped down my lemon-chewing-gum-flavored tea, and in the same hurried way I thought my conversation with Carmentxu had to some extent revealed the fact that I was scared. I'd gained nothing by having shown my cards so clearly; I felt absurd. That morning, on learning of the possible layoffs, I'd been overcome by the need to *do something about the situation*, but the situation was nothing more than a handful of rumors, and workers sticking to routine. When I left Carmentxu's office, I decided to go back down floor-by-floor, and talk to the people I knew. I hadn't gotten any clear information, much less *done something about the situation*. My detective zeal did, nonetheless, produce a low level of self-delusion.

I took the bus. It had been over a month since I'd caught a city bus home, and I noticed some of the boutiques whose windows used to catch my attention had closed. On Cibeles and the Gran Vía, I had the impression that there were fewer statues ranged along the façades of buildings. I couldn't have said which were missing. I thought the nervous anxiety that had been dragging me along for months was making me perceive things abnormally.

5

Despite the fact that they had just split up, for some days the tender tone of the conversations between Susana and her ex had been slipping through Skype well into the night. The Janssen she was now showing me on the screen of her laptop looked almost identical to the one I'd met. He was even wearing the same tartan hat—a bit tacky for my taste—he'd had in Madrid.

"Are you going to get back together?" I asked.

"Not sure."

I sat quietly, waiting for her to add something more. She opened a Word document and showed me some of the notes that, as she had once informed me, she made each day on her computer. They were very brief, more appropriate for jotting in a notebook given the haste with which they appeared to have been conceived, than for typing into the HP Mini she hauled around everywhere, and which took forever to boot up. I read a few, without giving them my full attention; my roommate's proximity, and the fact she maybe expected me to comment on them prevented me from concentrating.

"My idea is to combine the notes with photographs from Utrecht," she said, and opened the pictures folder. "See, that's me five years ago," she added.

I looked at the image: a Susana with bangs and long straight hair, wearing an outfit that reminded me of the uniforms they have in El Corte Inglés department store.

"It's from when I was working as a hotel receptionist," she informed me.

In Utrecht, she continued, she'd been an assistant in a preschool, a chambermaid, a private Spanish teacher, a nanny, and a kitchen assistant. In addition—and here her face lit with enthusiasm—she'd spent some time administering surveys, which meant traveling around the whole of the Netherlands. It was apparently tough work, because, despite her super-white skin, her foreign accent hampered that ritual of seduction all such interviewers have to deploy at point-blank range in order not to have doors slammed in their faces. That was the job she recalled with the most gratitude, since it had offered her the chance to really find out about Holland. You can only get an adequate understanding of such a reserved people, she said, by going into their homes. She told me her work as a chambermaid and kitchen assistant had put her in contact with people too, but not in the same way. In those jobs communication was limited to brief, repetitive exchanges. As always, Susana spoke very quickly, with gestures so exaggerated they lost all their communicative function, and allowed a glimpse of a particular state of mind that might have involved a degree of chaos, or insecurity, or both. If my feelings toward her were no longer quite so negative, I was still not sure I actually liked her. I attempted to match her experiences with my unfinished PhD, my time in Paris, my master's degree, and my work in publishing. I added that during the four months I spent living on a miniscule scholarship in the suburbs of Paris, I'd felt poor for the first time, in a way I didn't feel poor now, despite the fact I was only staying afloat due to her contribution to the rent. Perhaps it hadn't just been the lack of money that had made me feel that way in Paris, but also, and more importantly, that I didn't know anyone, it rained constantly, and there was often something hostile in the air. Susana interrupted and, as if she hadn't heard my words, told me that whirlwind of jobs had caused problems in her relationship with Janssen, because she'd been gradually wiping herself out, feeling increasingly exhausted, as if she were selling herself, and had begun to consider Janssen just one more obligation to be fulfilled.

That Susana gave such an extensive description of her working life in Holland that evening, yet still wouldn't say a word about her job in Madrid, changed my view of her. For a few days I expected that her opening up would mean an end to her secrecy, but no. During the last weeks, that appeal to cultural topics whenever she felt cornered had become more noticeable. One Saturday, something went wrong with the toilet, and while the plumber was explaining the correct way to pull the lever to avoid more serious repairs, my roommate interrupted—not without blinking weirdly and nodding impatiently first—to talk about a scene from

Ingmar Bergman's *Hour of the Wolf.* The plumber shrugged. Not long afterward, when I again began to take an interest in her working conditions (I was thinking of accepting any job that would imply a paycheck at the end of the month; I'd had some extra expenses that day, and the date of the last deposit in my checking account was well below the unending list of debits, written in red), I took advantage of another of those moments of expansiveness to try to wheedle information about her job from her. She was in the kitchen, preparing something for her dinner, and, looking at me in astonishment, she started talking about *Julie & Julia,* a movie I had seen. Without allowing her to finish, I said that I, like Julie, was a frustrated office worker, except that these days, my desk was covered in lentil husks and breadcrumbs by noon, and I had to put my padded Coronel Tapiocca jacket over my knees to ward off the cold. Unlike residential and office blocks, the building had no centralized heating system running through its main arteries reaching those smaller veins that come to the surface when circulation is low, warming and swelling the limbs. My bones were always exposed to the elements. I added that I was losing my inhibitions about working in a call center if it would offer me a steady income, and mean I didn't have to spend my days alone in the apartment. I said all this with a degree of dread because—when I thought about it—the idea of a daily commute and obligatory relationships with colleagues made me anxious. And then, would her company take on an overqualified applicant, or would I have to alter my CV? Initially, Susana appeared not to have heard me, but after a few seconds she said, "It's not worth talking about any of that." I didn't insist. Her attitude sent me back to the dark closed room of my timidity and suspicion.

6

Except for the occasional weekend away, I usually left the apartment after dark, which meant my encounters with the guys from the truck became almost routine. I continued to haunt the old prison, which had become a forest of rubble, a steep forest through which cockroaches scurried, and at night emitted a false glow—what in fact glimmered on the rubble were the lights from the Avenida de los Poblados. But it was as if those Dantesque fragments had light bulbs within them. I'd scramble through a hole in the wire fence and stay there quietly for a long time. I had the feeling that place was armor-plated, that it was enduring. The flood-lights that had once picked out the shadows of the prisoners had been dismantled, and I didn't dare explore the ruins in case I fell. So I walked around them. Fear didn't catch me; if large suburban parks like the Casa de Campo were being abandoned, with even the criminals going to places where they could get their hands on something more than hard carob beans and verbena petals, what was so different about that awkward heap of rubble? Before they pulled down the prison, I'd discovered that some of the cells—hardly much larger than six feet by four, and in which you couldn't take two turns without feeling dizzy—were occupied. They had posted a security guard so the panopticon didn't end up as a Romany village, but at night he turned a blind eye to a few solitary down-and-outs. In the occupied cells, I found the belongings of their nocturnal lodgers; everything had been extracted from dumpsters, which made the sight of over-coats and blankets on spindly hangers rather paradoxical. At that time, I had gone to the prison with a girlfriend who was making recordings of the silence in the center of the penitentiary. If my friend had been with me now, it would have been impossible for her not to register the sounds of that deformed urban skeleton and its creaky joints. But, back then it was as if we were in a tomb, with the crypts blocking out the hum of traffic. And now she would also have been able to record the guys from the truck, whom I'd seen stop by the wire fence one day, negotiate the gap, and snoop around with strong flashlights. They didn't see me. I was far off, quietly hunched down out of sight; there was a candy wrapper on the ground at my feet, and I could hear the chirping of insects. The third night I saw them playing daredevils on rotten planks, I realized they were looking for something that wasn't cardboard. My discovery should have been no surprise, but then I know nothing of the criminal underworld. What I did know was certain materials were being stolen for resale on the black market. Copper mostly. Yet it didn't ring true for me that, after years of standing empty, there would be anything of any value left in the prison. I don't know exactly what they were pilfering, but expected to see them carrying long, sharpened sticks, weapons. I felt the need to stand up, and as I did brushed against some piece of corrugated iron that fell with a loud clang. The five Romanies turned, and shone their flashlights in my direction; my knees were shaking slightly, and although I very much wanted to hunch down again, I couldn't even manage to breathe. They stood very still, making sweeps with their lights. The only things behind me were wire fencing, trees, and darkness. "Who's there?" they shouted, followed by, "If you don't get out of here, I'll slash you." Another one of them answered, "It's a cat or some dumbass. Let's go." The following day a number of front loaders turned up and cleared the area. What was left looked like a morass of gritty sand. I went back one last night, without being able to find the center of the lot, because I suddenly felt vulnerable, with too much city on either side and on the horizon. I stayed close to the wire fence with its geometric design, and farther on, to those kind of ungrounded tongs that emerged from the darkness in the park. That night, I made my way home with a clear head, following a new route. I amused myself by zigzagging left and right, sometimes taking long detours because I liked going along unknown streets. I'm not sure just when I found myself in a stretch of neighborhood I knew.

7

I had an unusual knack for orienting myself. It was an instinct that had been with me since childhood, and had nothing to do with drawing maps in my head. Whenever I consulted a map, I got lost. I never remembered the order of the streets, and wasn't concerned with finding that order. My free time was limited, and my aim was to shake off the sluggishness of my days, and also to reinvigorate my muscles, my bones, as if it were possible to give them back the vitality so many hours sitting quietly in a chair had bruised. That taut, dry skin I stretched while running, that skin from which I vainly tried to erase the wrinkles, was the real cartography. There are other ways to smooth or breathe energy into the chassis, like sex, but I'd given up on carnal relationships, so those runs I was scarcely aware of were useful for doing something with my body. If I got short of breath, I'd stop and look around (I always went to open spaces, since I spent the whole day longing to stretch my eyes; never crowded places, because I didn't like to be seen in a tracksuit, even if it was only by strangers); then I'd return by different streets and avenues, which reinforced my confidence in my ability to orient myself. I could rarely have said exactly where I was—at times the sense of being lost was complete. The undulating streets were misleading, and I'd feel I'd already gone a long way, but that didn't stop me from continuing. Eventually a sense of unease would force me to take note of my surroundings, and vaguely familiar doorways, stores, and squares would appear. I was never frightened by not knowing where I was, by the abandoned streets, the groups of unsavory teenagers, or the Latino Kings with their shiny yellow sparkle, because the petty thieves went downtown, and the Latino gangs were always fighting among themselves. I don't suppose I was much to look at anyway. My cheap, not particularly sporty sportswear, the clink of my keys, my face reddened by exertion, my hair drawn back in a ponytail, the freezing night. "Hey kid," someone had shouted at me once, since in that clothing, with my hair hanging any which way on the back of my neck, I'm not so different from an unattractive girl going to the all-night drugstore for her mother's medication—something I my-self did between the ages of sixteen and seventeen, when my mom was home sick: grabbing the prescriptions while my father imparted calm. The fact that I wasn't so different led me unwillingly to this conclusion: the passing of time changes nothing, we're constantly doing the same things, but we disguise them so they feel different. I didn't like us-ing my iPod; the songs became an isolating wall of noise, and it was like being inside a capsule that blocked out the elemental sounds. If I was in a capsule, it was perhaps made up of the walls of the apartment, the walls I wore during my runs like an invisible cape.

8

During one of my nocturnal runs I noticed how many of the houses in the neighborhood were squats. I went up Peñaflor and Hoya to an area that, despite all my meanderings, I didn't usually frequent because the steep streets meant it took time to reach any open sky, and what I was seeking out were views and quiet places. But that night I needed to wear myself out; I'd spent two days stuck in a badly compiled bibliography, containing entries that were difficult to check. I'd even had to make calls no one was going to reimburse me for. I'd had to search so hard for certain books I was toying with the idea that the essayist, in an attempt to support his argument, had purposely chosen nonexistent works by rarely translated Russian and Swedish authors, impossible to trace on the Internet. Maybe, I told myself, the strategy of some academics is to utilize invented sources to back up viewpoints the experts didn't agree with, because nothing has any solidity if not accompanied by endless references that all say the same thing. And it might even be that those sources have for decades only existed in footnotes. And what if the manipulation of those sources also endowed the academic with unlimited power, since no one denies the existence of something they have only heard of secondhand, not confessing they have been unable to access the text in case that admission lowers their prestige? The situation: the sidewalk was narrow, high, and awkward, like the ones in small towns, but once I'd checked that there were no cars around, it was simple to step into the street and reach the top of the hill, trying to beat my record of a hundred yards without stopping. What I found was another low hill, and then another, and another; from the manner they were disposed, it seemed as if space had a different density; I thought I'd never before seen hills that trick, not with their labyrinthine layout, as used to happen in Arab cities, but by having a space whose real extension retreated just when it was promising a panorama. I stopped; I was out of breath and slightly annoyed. I had neither gained the prize of being able to rest my eyes on an open vista, nor did I know what was there, farther on. The seventies subsidized housing projects alternated with low-rise houses that made me think of the towns in Ciudad Real. On one of those houses, some planks had been nailed across the door. It was a typical example of a building that had been closed up for years, and I would have continued to believe that was the case if a pot-bellied cat hadn't appeared in a crack in the slats, trying to squeeze the rest of its body through, and meowed at me. When it disappeared, I noticed a light filtering through the slats. I bent down, peered through the crack, and saw a hallway and, farther back, the shining orange bars of an electric heater, around which some feet were moving. The house was occupied, and the planks were there to disguise that fact. The following week, on a nearby street, I saw several houses that had been occupied in the same discreet way, with boards not quite doing the job and windows blocked with cardboard. From some of the buildings still under construction, cables led to nearby streetlamps, stealing electricity. If these acts of robbery took place so openly, it must mean the police and neighbors knew about them. I thought about the guys from the truck; I'd always assumed they lived in some form of clandestine housing, associated with illegal activity. I entered this new area of dwellings with stolen electricity; the gardens were nothing but bare earth, and only the sound of cars pierced a darkness whose destiny it was to disappear, to turn a corner into another unattractive square from which mystery would flee. I was aware of the existence of houses without zoning permits, and that there were many apartments left unfinished due to lack of funds, but I'd always thought those failed projects were located in the middle of bleak high plains, or at the distance from the coast specified in the regulations. I'd never imagined such things existed in the city. Perhaps this unfinished neighborhood had no official status. And it was also impossible to tell whether the apartments were illegally occupied, or cooperative dwellings inhabited by squatters despite being under construction still. Thinking over what had happened in recent years, the possibilities were endless: ghost housing projects, whole streets of empty downtown buildings whose owners didn't rent them in order to keep prices high by exploiting the shortage of available housing (the lower floors were offices or businesses, and the streets were bustling with an activity that seemed to contaminate even the rooftops crammed with billboards); some older buildings the city authorities had bought and allowed to be occupied because, while they still hoped to renovate them, there wasn't even enough in the coffers for adequate maintenance. On one occasion there had been a story in the press about a homeless family who had decided to finish off the construction of a detached house themselves so they could actually move in. The members of this family were famous for a couple of weeks, and newspapers and café conversations began to mention the phenomenon of self-construction, a practice that dated back to the postwar era. On the other hand, the historical buildings downtown had suffered from termite infestations for decades, and as it would be both difficult and expensive to repair the whole structure, metal columns had begun sprouting up everywhere, making the buildings look as though they were being constructed all over again in an old photograph. Although no building had actually fallen down due to these infestations, I once heard some had sunk noticeably. I imagined the ladies in the semi-basement apartments, peeling the potatoes for a roast, watching their windows being covered in cold mud, with its dense earthy odor, redolent of raw meat, and above it a strip of light and the street. I guessed the inhabitants of such apartments had been warned something of the sort might happen, and when it did they behaved like people living at the foot of a volcano, who spend years with one eye on the slender threads of smoke rising into clear skies: without any fuss, they gathered together their favorite clothes and their laptops. Despite the dishonesty of the co-ops, the downtown streets with their empty buildings, and the half-finished housing projects, until recently there hadn't been any protests. Those affected waited politely for a judgment while living with their parents or grandparents, and the ones who, with their own hands, tiled the bathroom walls of the house they had just purchased posed in resignation for the cameras of television news crews. The city remained more or less the same, with its appearance of organized chaos, of disaster borne. I sometimes used to go up to the fifth floor of the library where I worked when I tired of being in the apartment, although my visits became less frequent once they installed Wi-Fi, and I was no longer safe from the temptation of wasting time on the Internet. From its palatial windows, I'd observe the sunlit density of the air, which could include—near the M-30 or M-40 beltways—the slap of the city when you recalled it from the beach, because that panorama was a pure memory, and also a general impression of isolation, as if the buildings were uninhabited or occupied by the desert. That bleak plateau feel of the city could only be refuted by the sounds from the street, and in the often-empty library, all you could hear was silence. Those vistas sent me back to the Internet to take another look at Antonio López García's paintings, with their delirious exactitude, their phlegm spat at existence. The city seemed frozen, not by the cold, but by light and heat. From the fifth floor, you never saw pedestrians below. Not that they weren't there, it was just impossible to see them. The solitariness of the tall buildings, the very effective precariousness with which a limited number of forms multiplied—like amoebas and other organisms did when a ray of light gave life to the oceans—made the view eradicate life, and everything functioned like a reverse of that origin, since the earth was drying up. What could be seen below the brick rectangle was just that: rough earth. And for that reason, I told myself, the painting I was looking for, that painting I was sure I'd seen, had simplified form to the point of resolving it into just a few lines.

I wandered aimlessly around the neighborhood—it was truly enormous—for a while, looking at the lights from the windows falling onto the gritty ground; at some point I began to feel like I was being watched, not from the apartments projecting those lights, but from the ones that were unlit. There was no way to check if I was being observed, because the area was cloaked in complete darkness, but the impression was strong, and I stealthily returned to the street. What did it matter if someone was taking the trouble to watch me when, in any case, the habit of showing a little of what you're thinking should be a common practice? I started running again; I was wearing my thick winter tracksuit, and wanted to project a less heavy image onto the store windows.

When I got back to the apartment, I found Susana sitting with a very slender, strangely beautiful pair of nail scissors, delicately slicing through an impressive brochure from the State Land-Use Institute containing a map of the city. She was leaning over the northern zone cutting out residential buildings not larger than half my thumbnail, plus—and this seemed to me some form of madness—cars the size of fleas, whose shapes, removed from the miniscule streets of the map, were reduced to specks of color. She worked with skill; it took her just three seconds to slide the scissors around each tiny image. She then put them in envelopes labeled "Trees," "Gardens," "Tall Buildings," "Small Buildings." Gradually, all that was left of the map was the street grid. This was the first time she'd done her cutting in the living room; every other night she went into her room to devote herself to her miniature clippings. I asked what she was up to, and she told me she wanted to relocate the buildings. Her aim was for the map to be just the same in terms of structure, but with all the various elements transposed. She was going to make a number of maps.

"Aren't there computer programs that can do it more quickly?"

"I guess so, but that has less charm for me," she said. "On the computer, I could get twenty different combinations in a few minutes. They'd be perfect, but I like to be able to see the work. The dirtiness."

"And what are you going to do with it all?"

Susana picked up the backpack containing her laptop, and took out a roll of maps.

"I want to make a series. Then I can burn them, or exhibit them," and when she pronounced the words "exhibit them," there was a spark in her eyes. That would give her an entrance into the cultural universe she was obsessed with, or at least utilized as a mask or a cuirass, or whatever. "There's a movie," she went on, "where an artist disassembles what he can see from his window on canvases. While breaking down one part of the scene, he begins to perceive his street just as it is in his paintings. He goes to the supermarket, which seems to have been ground in a mortar, and he picks up a jar of mayonnaise that looks like a Pringle chip. Everyone around him is behaving normally, and only the neighbor he's already carved into shades of ochre and gold merges into the new order. They chat politely; his neighbor's head cracks open above his nose, and a hand comes out and starts throwing cans of beer at the scouring pad that was once his shopping cart. The artist is pleased the world has obediently complied with his aesthetic principles. Then the movie goes downhill, and ends up being completely predictable."

I had no desire to ask just how it went downhill. What I wanted to do was crawl into my bed, but my roommate's eyes and magpie voice fixed me to the wall, as if they had stuck me there with thumbtacks. She went on to detail, down to the non-quantum mechanics, the rest of the movie. While she was recounting the plot (I thought she was inventing it; I'm not sure why, because she had seen almost every movie ever created and had an amazing memory), she cut out an area of Villaverde with white lancet Gothic buildings, like pointed leaves. She was using a magnifying glass, and the reflection played on the paper. I began to slide toward my bedroom door. I told her I wanted to work a while before going to sleep. She made space for me at the table.

"You can work here. We don't have to talk. And Janssen is online."

I glanced at the HP Mini and saw Janssen leaning over what appeared to be a book. For a moment, I imagined Susana at work, accompanied on-screen by her Dutch boyfriend or ex-boyfriend, with her computer at her feet so her boss wouldn't catch her, not saying a word. Janssen would be spying on her lower limbs in their thick black leggings. Susana was unable to disguise her anxiousness to have her laptop connected at all hours. Since she'd gotten partially back together with Janssen, the first thing she did when she returned to the apartment was to take the HP from her backpack and switch it on. While the motor emitted its metallic sound, she'd make herself comfortable and, before she'd even begun to lay into the baguette and the coffee I'd made, Janssen would be on the screen. They never wrote, and for some reason or other didn't chat either. Eventually the hour for using Skype to talk instead of just being there would come, but that was later, after Susana had finished her cutting out, her notes, her movies, and her virtual or real visits to exhibitions. Some nights Janssen wasn't home, and Susana would constantly check the screen as she snacked. She seemed tensed in a different way, with more passion and less rigidity, and I had the impression she was going to start singing some Flamenco soleá or fado, or a folk song. She was impatient when we talked; if Janssen appeared, she'd announce, "Here's Janssen," as if she'd just crossed off the last number on a bingo card. Our relationship had changed noticeably, and not because she stopped being evasive about her past and her job, it was more that living together had made us finally get used to each other, feel natural in the other's company. We didn't spy on each other. She was sitting across from me very quietly. I thought it must be the result of having spent the whole evening with her clippings, and that her boyfriend, or ex-boyfriend, had spent all day in a small square on the left of the screen, like a china doll in a store window. When I switched on my laptop I felt alone:

there was no one to accompany me in that way. I checked my inadequate, cold Facebook page. It also occurred to me I'd already spent a lot of time on my galleys that Sunday, and my supposed intention of working through the night had been a white lie that was beginning to look gray. I held out for forty-five minutes. Then, with the excuse that I couldn't keep my eyes open, managed to go to my room. When I got into bed, I realized I was shivering.

9

A few days later, when I was on the street, I experienced
a sudden sense of foreboding, a runaway premonition, an
absolute chaos of my nervous system. I noticed that the
store where the year before I'd ordered an exercise bike had
closed. Bankrupt businesses are, I thought, minor details
in an organism whose heart is still beating at full capac-
ity, and shouldn't alarm me. That's what I said to myself
when I arrived at the Plaza de Aluche shopping mall, from
the dome of which snowflakes were being blown onto the
ashen street. There were signs advertising the January sales,
and the stores were full. Despite it being an everyday scene,
there was something not quite normal about the bustling
crowds, something reminiscent of outlying French boule-
vards, where the indecisive clientele take their time milling
in front of the store windows. I boarded a bus; I needed to
see more, and as the vehicle sped up everything around it
slowed down, as if the dogs were taking twice as long to sniff

corners and the trunks of plane trees. The only people not on the move were the retirees sitting on benches in the hazy sunshine, an ordinary scene, even if there did seem to be too many of them, and the way they were bunched together in certain squares, under statues and around particular official buildings, offered a different, distorted reading. For a few seconds those old people became monsters looking at me with cajoling smiles. It took me some time to find the appropriate words to express that perception, to recognize they were visions. I noted the throb of my pulse in my ears. And this thought also occurred to me: someone, or something, is sending me a warning. For a while I was poised on the verge of collapse.

The bus moved away from the parasites. I tried to speak. The blood wasn't reaching my hands and feet. They were cold, dry; they were going to detach themselves from my body. When I took a step, I couldn't feel the ground, and I grabbed at a woman's coat.

"Are you drunk?" she asked disapprovingly.

I managed to alight from the bus—there was still no ground under my feet, and I had to support myself against the buildings. Then I sat down in a doorway and stayed there for I don't know how long, until my sense of touch returned. It occurred to me that I was crazy. I formulated this thought ten, twenty times. I walked. Movement was painful. The lacerating rumble of traffic. The tense, high-pitched voices of friends chatting in doorways. The people walking behind me. Their breathing, their bodies, were too close. I was intolerable even to myself, wanted to tear my body to pieces. I got to the apartment and walked through all the rooms, including Susana's. Then I flopped onto the bed. I tried to brush away the sensation that a catastrophe was making me its epicenter, but everything continued to feel unreal. I started walking, slowly this time, around the apartment, went into the kitchen and looked at the stove; in the living room, I observed the old table and the shelves crammed with grubby books. Objects were giving off a heavy existence that was crushing me. I went back to bed and fell into an exhausted sleep.

I woke with a sense of helplessness and anxiety that was worse than my earlier perceptions. Or at least that's what I initially thought, but then I began to take control of myself, to find the energy to search for information about my unwelcome agitation on the web. I typed in schizophrenia, and then psychosis. I hadn't heard any voices; I'd seen masks. I asked myself, asked the screen, what the essence of my experience was. I found these two words, *panic attack*, and then I remembered the period when Germán used to faint during meetings. I called him.

"I'm having panic attacks," I said. "And I think I'm going mad."

It felt fabulous to talk, to weave phrases, and to name; amazing that my voice hadn't turned into the clatter of cans tied behind a wedding car.

The act of speech, installing an order, relaxed me, and I went on giving Germán different versions of the same situation: I'm having panic attacks, I think I'm going mad too.

"Stop, Elisa. They're just panic attacks. That's why you think you're going mad," he told me, or maybe I heard him for the first time, and he'd been repeating it all the while.

Then the following conversation took place, during which I was able to project a semblance of non-panic. I don't know where I got the strength, or who it was that was speaking:

"You told me you used to be paralyzed."

"That too. What have you read? Panic attacks take different forms. Do you want me to come over?"

"No."

"Well, I'll come this evening, anyway. After work. Doesn't Susana have any anxiolytics?"

"How would I know? Why?"

"Hasn't she told you anything?"

"She doesn't talk about herself. Only about her boyfriend or ex-boyfriend, and her weird art projects. You said she was normal."

"I didn't tell you that. I just said that someone used to sharing apartments wouldn't give you any trouble. Anyway, she is an odd sort of person, isn't she?"

"I don't want to talk about Susana right now."

"Sorry. I'll see you this evening."

When I hung up, something very light had settled back in its place. Then the buzzing silence returned. That buzz was several decibels louder than yesterday, than the day before yesterday, than a month ago. But I knew how to get rid of it. In a chest painted with rural scenes I had two bottles of wine, another two of whiskey, a Polish vodka, and the Orujo brandy a monk in Burgos had given me. I'd found the chest in the Salamanca neighborhood on one of the nights they collected discarded furniture, along with a few other minor gems eaten by woodworm.

Hang on to thought. In the past, whenever I'd been close to breaking point, I'd sought a *logical* way out. A way knowledge could guarantee. As if knowledge weren't a flimsy construction. I spent the time until Germán arrived looking on the Internet for the causes of my ailment, and for cures. I didn't eat anything, couldn't swallow, but I was back to myself again. Back to my incipient depression and my *logic*. It was eight when Germán turned up; Susana, who had returned from work at her usual hour and gone to her room, came out to say hello, and that was the first time I saw them together. They talked about people I didn't know, and it was unbearable to stand there with the smell of their shirts; I thought I was going to have another attack. I took a bottle of whiskey from the chest, and drank down half a glass neat. When I returned to the living room, Susana said, "Right, I'll leave you to talk."

She didn't disturb us. I could feel the drink coursing relief through my veins, while Germán warned me I'd feel worse the next day, that alcohol triggers panic after its initial positive effects. I couldn't have cared less: I was euphoric, overwhelmingly happy, with that tipsy conviction that a permanent state of bliss is possible. I stopped believing in what had happened. Germán had gotten hold of a packet of Xanax for me. After he left, I threw up, took a pill, and went to bed. When I got up, I took another, and checked the minimum recommended dosage online. I felt sleepy all day, but attempted to work on my galleys. While I didn't feel any panic, I wasn't well either, but it was a bearable not well.

Over the following days I went to the library to work, taking a couple of pints of tea with me, as I was incapable of spotting errors without a stimulant. Before leaving, I also swallowed two Xanax. The tea stopped me from staring out the window for too long, or going out to smoke; the pills kept the panic at bay. Although I was determined to be well, there was still the underlying feeling that everything could turn apocalyptic, and I was uneasy about spatial disposition and the looks of the librarians, feeling I might pass out before their eyes. I had no idea why that reaction disappeared when I concentrated. The Xanax ran out after a week. I hadn't had any more attacks, and thought that with a little more time, I'd achieve some level of stability. That notion lasted one day. The following morning I broke down again. I'd gone early to the office to drop off a manuscript; on the way back, I sat behind the bus driver. I noted a tingling in my legs and arms that seemed to be paralyzing me. It was as if it was all happening to someone else. I thought I was having a stroke, and that death must be a serene act of communion with one's scant strength.

"Can you get the driver to stop and call an ambulance? I can't move my arms," I said to the woman beside me, an Ecuadoran who, rather than carrying out my request, looked at me as if I were Marilyn Manson and got off the bus.

After a few minutes, I got movement back, and that's when fright kicked in. I managed to exit the bus, take refuge in a café, and call Germán, who came to pick me up in a cab. Irritating light, bustling crowds, harsh sounds. Mummies. My head swimming as Germán hugged me, and his warm skin softening the breakdown. I returned to a state just on the right side of pathological.

"The woman at work only had Lexotan," said Germán

when he could see I was calmer. "You need to see a psychiatrist. Let's make an appointment with your physician."

I nodded. My regular doctor saw me that same afternoon, and out of a sense of duty felt she had to reprimand me: Why on earth hadn't I told my family what was going on? Was I so proud I'd deprive my parents of their right to know about my state of health? She had those blond streaks with brown and gray roots that make you think of a dirty ashtray, purplish lips, and a scarf with a design more suitable for curtains than a fashion accessory. She gave me a prescription for more Xanax, a referral note for the psychiatrist, and a rubber ball you squeezed to calm your nerves. There was a waiting list of a week to see the psychiatrist.

I spent four days incapable of making any other decision than to hang in there until the anxiety passed, but the only things that went away were the shadow of the monster during daylight hours and the dark presences at night, milling around my bed, waiting to sink their claws into my cervical vertebrae. I finally mixed the Xanax with alcohol, and the anxiety abated a little, but I couldn't drink much if I wanted to work. The only time I overdid it was the day I had to collect a manuscript from the office. I've no idea what state I was in when I arrived, or what Carmentxu thought. And although I'd crossed the whole city to get there, I was still unable to make use of that outing to go to the hospital. Writing this, I now realize something inside me was clinging to my state of collapse.

Germán stopped me from blowing off my appointment with the psychiatrist. The day I was scheduled to see him, I decided not to show up, but Germán called me a couple of hours before the appointment, and when I blurted out my determination not to leave the apartment, he came around, forced me to get dressed, and bundled me into his car. I think Susana, whom I'd been hiding from the whole week, asked something along the lines of, "Anything wrong?" and Germán told her he'd call later. I was in such a state about having to go outdoors, I didn't take in what they were saying.

In the psychiatrist's office, the trembling started again, and my jaw began to make all sorts of spasmodic jerks. As far as I remember he scarcely spoke to me, just injected a tranquilizer and handed Germán a prescription. I slept for sixteen hours after the injection; when I woke, there were two packets of pills on my bedside table, and underneath them a piece of paper with instructions written in Germán's cramped handwriting. The curative cocktail was composed of tranquilizers and antidepressants. I took them. I spent the whole morning curled up in the fetal position, and when Susana returned from work, she repeated the instructions Germán had written down, adding:

"You have to go back to the psychiatrist next week. If you don't want me to go with you, Germán can. He said to call him."

In that state, like someone suffering from narcolepsy, I could hardly do any proofreading, so I phoned my boss and said I had a temperature of a hundred and four. The chemically induced somnolence, with its unpredictable cycles, kept me in a state of false calm during which I occasionally managed to be an almost normal person who had gotten up with a hangover, regretting the stupid behavior of the night before.

Susana asked me each day if I'd taken my pills. She used to observe me with an air of serenity; maybe my weakness made her feel safe. She made an effort to convince me I'd been lucky, that crises can be absolutely devastating. I asked what she meant, but she didn't explain.

One evening she came in and put my book on the bedside table. She'd borrowed it from the library. Between the pages she'd inserted the short story, or whatever you would call it, I'd written for the newspaper, as if she was compiling an anthology of my collected works. That crumpled story with its prescient description of trajectories and falls seemed to me cursed, and I asked her to remove it from the table.

"I thought seeing what you'd done would give you strength," she said in apology, as if she were a self-help manual.

"I'm grateful for the thought, but the truth is it upsets me," I lied.

What was bothering me was Susana observing my reaction to jeopardy. Now, every physical object, including the book, was shrouded in an aura of existing in another dimension. And if I opened the novel and read a couple of pages? What kind of nonsense would those words form?

10

During a course I enrolled in after moving to Aluche, when I was mulling over the idea of starting up a publishing services company, they taught us the keys to time management in business; that is to say, doing things in a purposeful way, without thinking about coffee breaks or the beautiful but horrendous landscape of a brick-building neighborhood. The arguments included in the class were supported by scientific studies carried out in American universities that demonstrated the inefficiency, and resulting increased stress levels, of going, as I do, straight from between the sheets to the computer, with a dozen trips to the kitchen or checks of email before returning to bed. The studies included experiments in which freelancers were made to spend weeks in ghostly looking lofts, with no access to social networks, or anything besides their clients' deathly dull web pages. Their output increased significantly. I made an effort to translate that code into pages and word counts, but sweat, an aching back, cooking oil, dust, my respiration, the images each lexical item or sentence generated all got in the way. It was impossible to convert my activities into pure action. Thanks to the enforced discipline of the experiment, the freelancers in those American university studies (Trevor Harris, Doron Nissim, Robert Herz, Morgan Stanley, Jerome A. Chazen, Gauri Bhat, Ryan Wilson) who, like me, had previously worked very late into the evening seven days a week, were able to finish their tasks in the late afternoon, and take Saturdays and Sundays off. During the course, we did some exercises designed to give us an approximate experience of the levels of efficiency achieved by a good dose of willpower. There were days when I tried to follow those guidelines, summarized on a piece of blue paper in one of my drawers. True, by sticking to them, I was able to finish the work I'd scheduled for the day earlier; however, everything still left to be done the following days only reminded me of how alone and frustrated I was. My anxiety levels then rose a sufficient number of notches to make free time undesirable. By contrast, the constant activity, sautéed with the strange depths of nothingness on the Internet, paradoxically increased the possibility of forgetting my situation. That sense of evasion was no big deal, although it did increase my anger, and the feeling of having had it up to here, so I'd get to the end of the day with my adrenaline pumping. And then I enjoyed my walks.

But what happened was that my volume of work began to increase because they were giving me more books to correct with very short deadlines, and that meant making an even greater effort, with some working days finishing not at nine or ten, but midnight. Despite the fact that they had begun to pay me for those urgent books, I was still owed for earlier jobs. Sometimes I thought about the win-win negotiation strategies I'd also learned in that course aimed at teaching freelancers to make the most of their autonomy. I wasn't really in a position to offer concessions, but I managed to work out a few strategies that might persuade Carmentxu that my continued loyalty benefited us both. I did this with a solicitousness I'd never displayed while working in the office, but obtained neither any form of remuneration, nor personal satisfaction for my pains. Week after week I left my boss's office humiliated not only by my increasing penury but also by something I had difficulty admitting to. The Grupo Editorial Término's fiction imprint published works by best-selling authors, and the literary greats. Although I didn't belong in either category, and for a long time had been saying that my vision of myself as a writer had been just a chimera, it hurt me that my boss had never shown the slightest interest in what I'd done, and what I perhaps might do in the future. At heart, I'd never resigned myself to occupying the humble position of proofreader, and still thought things might come together again so that one day I'd be able to write another book, and so gain a stronger reputation. From the time I'd become an independent contractor and my spirits sunk to rock bottom, that circumstance, which in the past had scarcely bothered me, had been growing into a central aspect of my disquiet.

11

"How old are you?"

"Forty-four," replied Susana.

I looked at her in astonishment. There wasn't a single wrinkle on her face, her body didn't sag in the wrong places; her enormous Wagnerian breasts were firm, even when she wasn't wearing a bra, and despite the fact that she was definitely large, and liked to eat, she had no mountainous bulges. I'd seen her in her underwear a couple of times, and her ass, of the same proportions as the rest of her and shaped weirdly like a packing box, was athletic, as if she spent three hours a day doing rhythmic gymnastics and took shots of anabolic steroids.

"I was late starting everything. I began to train as a teacher late, tried to specialize late, and my longest relationship was late in coming too. Before college I spent some time in London, and then I went to Colombia, and graduated in Cali. I took three courses in psychology. They were early morning classes. One day I overslept, and when I arrived on the campus there was a shoot-out going on. Some of my classmates died. That's when I had my psychotic episode. I saw them collecting the bodies and cleaning up the blood. Thirty-two people killed. What do you think of that? The next day I began to have the feeling someone was watching me: outside the window, on the bus, from the television screen. And then my name was mentioned on the news: the only student at the university they had really wanted to kill had gotten away. I was sharing an apartment with two girls, one from England and the other from Portugal, who volunteered with me at an organization that helped street children, and they were concerned because I was spending the whole day in my room, playing Frank Zappa and not sleeping. The children under my care wanted to know what was wrong. But in my room, I was thinking of them as gremlins in human disguises. I have only very vague memories of all this; I'd have believed it was all a dream if my roommates hadn't been able to confirm some of my delusions. Of course, I wouldn't have forgotten those delusions, but they belonged to a weird order of things. I was committed in a psychiatric clinic for three weeks, until my sister turned up. Over the following six months, I took Risperdal because I was wrongly diagnosed as being schizophrenic. Then I went on lithium. The Risperdal made my head shake, and I had the sensation I was swaying all the time. And the tics extended to my tongue: it felt like one of those spongy dishcloths soaked in water. I was giving poetry readings, and with every verse my neck would jerk back, as if it had been struck by a force ten gale. I had to stop the readings because I got torticollis, but the psychiatrist and the psychologist kept telling me I must keep up with my regular activities. Strange to say, the pharmaceutical company that manufactures Risperdal is called Janssen, and they have a Colombian branch. Before coming back to Spain, my sister and I decided to travel around for a while. What I believe now is that she took away my medication and left me to hallucinate throughout the whole trip. I hardly remember anything about that time. Just olive green jungle, and guerillas transporting cocaine, asking about Susana Baños, the student who had escaped the shoot-out. To be honest, I don't really know if my sister did take me traveling. It could have been a hallucination mixed with things I saw on TV in Colombia. I never asked her because I was off my head for months, and I preferred my version. The Risperdal also made me suffer insomnia, and I was always hungry. I put on forty-five pounds, and then lost them on the Atkins diet. And I spent a lot of time with my mouth open because my nostrils were always dry, and I was overproducing saliva. I was a fantastic sight."

Susana continued with her stream of events, telling me that on her return to Spain she started putting ads for partners in the classified sections of newspapers. And thanks to one of those ads, she had a relationship with a dwarf. She told me every detail of that relationship without blushing. She'd never talked so much about herself before, and I had the impression my anxiety was seeping into her words.

Over the following days I stopped experiencing the drowsiness and morbid jumpiness of chemical shock. But what my roommate had told me was making me increasingly uneasy.

This now seems to be another consequence of my crisis: for a few days I managed to forget about what had happened to me, because I could only think about Susana. And the dwarf. I don't know if it was some form of evasion, or simply life going on between the fear and the pills. I say life because, for the first time in three years, I had the desire to write, and I gave myself up unreservedly to that impulse.

I constructed a short story around Susana's tale, attempting to capture the impression her words had made on me: a mixture of fascination and astonishment.

I didn't want to use my laptop because the screen reminded me too much of work, so I wrote in a notebook. When I finished I had no idea how to judge it. I was obsessed with the idea of making the structure clear. The similarity between my voice, included in brackets, and Susana's was a serious concern; when I reread it, I speculated that this was not the result of incompetence on my part, but of direct evidence. It also seemed to me that the narrative rested on the ease and lightness with which everything was resolved, and also expressed my own nostalgia for the era when I was growing up: the eighties. There had been no junkies in my family to water down the myth. I saw myself at the age of eleven or twelve in the living room at home, gripped by my earliest problems, focused on how the characters in television series and books dealt with the repercussions of rape, infidelity, or failure in the blink of an eye.

In the psychiatrist's office, I didn't mention the manuscript, or my obsession with Susana's story, but limited myself to telling him about my toxic trip, and from the impatience of his nods, I imagined Germán must have already informed him of all that.

The psychiatrist, a fat, aged man who patted his thighs as he spoke, told me that the state of anxiety is the summit of some type of contradiction over which he had been trekking for many years, a contradiction that, just like a cancer, if not removed at an early stage, will metastasize and spread to every aspect of life, to every small decision, to perception, to the air.

Then he explained the stages of the treatment, recommended I didn't work until I'd stabilized on the medication, and asked me to write a letter about my work, specifying what I put into it, what I got back, what I hoped for, and how I organized my life. I had to bring the letter to the next session. He added that when I was feeling better, he would send me to see a therapist.

I made a mental calculation of my savings; I could get by for two more months. When I was about to stand and leave the room, the psychiatrist said, "The young man who was with you told me you're a published author."

I suppose I gave him a weary look. It passed through my mind to relate my problem with writing, but what really occurred to me had nothing to do with that, but with myself. Writing was one more scenario in my fear.

"I don't have what it takes," I said.

12

Susana hadn't mentioned her confession again, and I had no desire to inquire further. Deep down, I was terrified by what she'd told me, and what I'd written based on it. I realized my worries were also rooted in the expectation that her tale would contain something that might help me. The mood, the defiance underlying her story, set my nerves on edge because it was beyond my reach. I was incapable of applying it to myself. I felt too broken to admit distances, and too close to a form of madness I couldn't explore without horror.

Her behavior was very much as normal: silence alternating with movie plots. She had thought up a strategy for regaining Janssen's errant attention. When she was telling me about her plan, it was as if something in her throat had had to go in search of her voice. She used to speak to Janssen on Skype almost every day, she told me, but as her boyfriend or ex-boyfriend's appearances were now becoming less frequent, she suspected he was seeing other women.

"He's trying to decide if it's worth all the fuss of breaking up with me for good."

"And do you want to go on with someone who's doing that?"

"I'm not sure. And even if I was, I've told you what I'm like."

And that was the only reference she made to her confession, which now seemed to be dispersing like clouds that sudden gusts of wind shred until they are flecks, or white horses on waves, scudding across a blue that always glimmers. Susana had decided to pretend to be interested in other men, not by her absence, which would have been impossible, but by dropping a series of hints on social networks. According to her, she had somehow, almost without realizing it, begun virtual flirtations, but in a way that only existed in her head. She asked me to add her on Facebook, and allow her to view herself from my page. I had no idea how that was different from viewing herself on her own wall, if in the end her picture and words were the same, and anyway the idea was to make Janssen jealous. Susana answered that viewing herself among the profiles of strangers did make a difference. I wanted to respond that her contacts viewed her own timeline, not mine, but was afraid she would interpret this observation as a refusal to acquiesce. In spite of the fact that the chemicals were beginning to take effect, making me calmer, quieter, I was experiencing a strong fear of conflict, of taking the lid off a pan and finding myself faced with a frog. I didn't trust the medication. I added her name to my friends, without commenting that her username (Karfloggyari) didn't seem particularly suited to her purpose, and neither did her photograph, showing only her horrendously huge thick-rimmed glasses and a peevish expression. In her photo gallery there were no images of the clippings that, with the patience of those people who do jigsaw puzzles, she used to construct the pieces of the disordered Madrids. But there were photographic miniatures that Facebook, and perhaps Susana herself in turn, had made even smaller. Some of those miniatures were like dots in an ocean of white, and it was no use enlarging them to get a better look, since the outlines then dissolved into shadows. Just like the images she worked with on paper, you had to hold a magnifying glass to the screen.

I'd already had more than enough of Susana's clippings, which she kept in three-ring binders gummed to sheets of thick paper. But from time to time I'd find a thumbnail-sized store clerk, a sixty-something swimmer standing thigh-deep in water, a dishwasher, a rose bush, a metal whisk under the sofa, and only then would I remember the images on the kitchen and bathroom walls, which had become such an integral part of daily life they were almost invisible. When I came across one of Susana's clippings, I'd hold it next to the two women like Siamese cats in the living room to check out the effect, and sometimes also to play, as if there were a doll's house with its tiny inhabitants on my wall. Having Susana on Facebook led me to examine her contact list for overlaps, or search for the sister she mentioned the night she told me about her manic periods. The only things those contacts revealed were the generation she belonged to and her past life in Utrecht. There was a large percentage of Svens, Sems, Toms, and Stijns, who must surely be Dutch, and friends and acquaintances of Janssen, which made my roommate's plan of making him jealous pretty unviable. Susana checked Facebook a couple of times a day from my account, although she rarely looked at her own. She would amuse herself with my contacts—for the most part from the publishing world and constantly talking about books. She eavesdropped on their conversations and added comments. Every so often I went into her timeline and read her posts in English and the comments she made on others'; I realized there was a man named Antonio who won hands down in terms of likes. He was a redhead of indefinite age, connected with a company called Telcomark. I clicked on the name, thinking it was perhaps Susana's employer, and found that it was indeed a telemarketing business. My roommate's silence about her work was still complete. I didn't have the slightest idea where she went every morning when I'd theoretically not yet opened my eyes, even though I was in fact awake, and only waiting for her to leave before getting up. That early-morning Susana, whose movements I imagined from my bed, seemed a stranger to me, and I related her with the unbearable, terrifying Susana of those first days. My anxious imagination refused to unshackle itself from everything that generated dread; in my dreams it almost mythologized her. During the day, her ghost would be gradually divested of its terrifying aspects, and in the evening came the coffee (decaf for me), conversation, and reading her messages to Antonio on Facebook. I fantasized about what might be going through Janssen's mind when he saw Susana flirting on that social network, and I wondered how she managed to be attractive, despite all her freakishness and the lack of self-esteem that, at times, due to her strength of will, seemed to me inauthentic. I sometimes imagined Janssen masturbating to sexualized scenes in which Susana and Antonio played the lead roles. Susana was by that time posting images of herself in swimwear, with that talent she had for making the most of her Dantesque body, like an advertisement for Dove vindicating the rights of *real* women through that tool that allows supreme fictions about oneself. Under the photos, Antonio wrote, "Mmmmmmm."

13

After a few weeks on the medication my mood lifted. I started working again, and went outdoors to savor the extraordinary pleasure of passing unnoticed amid the crowd without a trace of the monster. Nevertheless, while the evidence that words and thought are a bodily chemical gave me a sense of triumph, everything was reconfigured to include distortion again, the not seeing what was happening. The effects certain events should produce were erased. Perhaps those effects were just a fiction I imagined. One morning before getting down to work, I read in the newspaper that my company was about to hold a creditors' meeting as a measure for avoiding bankruptcy. This would probably mean consternation in the offices, picketers outside, an unprecedented minor commotion, all of which made me look for an excuse to be there. When I arrived, I found the usual high-level efficiency, as if nothing had happened and I'd gotten it all wrong. I wasn't even capable of worming my way into the whispering around the coffee machines, as it felt intrusive. The following day, an anonymous email message appeared in my inbox indicating the date of the creditors' meeting. If that took place, my payments would be delayed even further, or I might perhaps never receive anything at all. I'd been punctually paid for the urgent books, and the latest news seemed contradictory. A few days went by during which, when I wasn't rewriting my manuscript, I answered the chain of emails generated by the original message. In the end, I got fed up with my suppositions and the emails. I chose my clothes carefully: a gray jacket I'd inherited after my mother's death, black cropped pants, black pumps with medium heels; a slight transformation that should raise me a few inches above my tendency for silence. I also checked if Carmentxu would be available: on the last few occasions I hadn't managed to see her, and was beginning to suspect she was making herself scarce to avoid having to offer me any explanation; and as I'd been promptly paid for the urgent books, I hadn't really wanted to dig any deeper. But I wasn't earning enough to return to my old life on Plaza Tirso de Molina, so the balm was only effective when compared to the months with absolutely no income. I was aware those maneuvers were no threat. Carmentxu was just an employee, but accessing the ghostly executives above her was a pipe dream, and I'd decided to protest in my own way. I told her I was having difficulties with a memoir by the widow of a postwar Spanish writer, which needed to be rewritten. While the widow was competent in terms of narrative, now that she was older she found it hard to string the paragraphs together. It had been fifty years since the writer's death. During the previous two weeks, I'd been working on the task of organizing and polishing the amalgam of hand-written and typed sheets covered in Wite-Out and crossings out, written by a ninety-year-old woman who often forgot what she had said ten lines earlier. I had plenty of questions, all of which could have been sent by email, but I wanted to spend enough time in Carmentxu's office to make her uncomfortable. At heart, what I wanted was to escape from the circularity of those months, and enter the realm of possibility. Breaking the links in that chain required a set of favorable circumstances, anger, or an explosion of emotion that would loosen the knots of my rationality and moderation.

I appeared in her office, and my voice sounded normal. We went through the pages of the manuscript together; Carmentxu was in a bad mood following an argument with the wife of a Mexican sacred cow who refused to allow her husband to travel to Spain unless he flew business class, was given a suite at the Palace Hotel, and got a personal driver.

"Aren't there any eccentric husbands?" I asked.

"We haven't got any elderly female writers of that status. The only one whose husband made a nuisance of himself was snatched from us by Grupo Astro."

The widow of the postwar Spanish writer, who herself had penned a number of books of a pedagogic nature, lived in a small town in Ávila and, according to Carmentxu, was a darling. They sent a messenger to pick up the successive versions of the memoir, since they didn't trust the postal service and the widow didn't keep copies. As she'd said in an interview, she was seventy-five when the Internet appeared, with computers just a little earlier, and downright refused to allow her ocean of memories to be converted into a glare of pixels, because she suffered from dry eyes and frequent bouts of conjunctivitis. She wrote by hand, and occasionally on an old electric typewriter, without looking at the keys, her eyelids almost closed, and with a humidifier close to her face to alleviate the dryness. In the interview, she also said she applied artificial tears every half hour, "so I'm crying all day." It was the widow's most frequently visited piece on the web; the interviewer had come up with the sensationalist title "I Spend the Whole Day in Tears." But the interview itself was a bit of a let down: the widow was not in fact a tearful woman. During those two weeks I had spent transferring her text dealing with events that had taken place in Madrid onto the computer, I'd found it hard to avoid thinking of the colors and motifs of Ortega Muñoz's canvases, as if the widow's memories came not from the streets of the capital but from the lines of dead trees in those canvases, with their branches raised in supplication to the heavens, and also of rows of equally withered vines, and the everlastingly brown, gray, and yellowed parcels of fields, and the horizon barely visible through the clouds of dust over the plateau. These days the sun was still as strong, but the Madrid light was no longer clear; it was thick with smog. The brick-scape, the throng of buildings crowned by antennae, resembled Ortega Muñoz's countryside, or simply the countryside, without Ortega Muñoz. The brick was the same color as the earth around Madrid, which in turn was the same as the earth of the paintings of vines and gaunt trees, and I felt there might be some form of aesthetic rather than just material coherence between the buildings, resulting from progress and the art of some of the painters of that period. This misdirected idea allowed me to find an order in the disorder generally produced by what I saw from my window; the city of uncontrolled growth; a voracious, exorbitant, poor city.

Carmentxu was wearing a thin, low-cut top. The breeze, laden with exhaust from the M-30, alongside which the Grupo Término building stands, was strong enough to necessitate weighing down the papers strewn over desks with books and staplers while I was showing my editor the repetitive anecdotes I'd deleted from the widow's text. When we finished, I articulated my question in the manner of someone pulling a rabbit out of a top hat, naturally, and with ingenuous aplomb. There was always some previous agreement, which rarely admitted renegotiation, but I was behaving as if I were dumb.

"It means I have to spend extra time on the widow's memoirs. My contract doesn't cover that," I said.

I had the impression Carmentxu had no idea what I was talking about, not because of any lack of clarity on my part, but because it was inconceivable that I would be asking for more money. I was afraid she would scold me the way my mother used to with a "But, aren't you aware…?" giving shape to all those accusations that had made me feel idiotically guilty as a child for having done things badly without knowing why. My mother's recriminations had followed an apparently simple logic I didn't understand. Entering the adult world involved utilizing the mysteriously crushing rationales that invested the person employing them with power, while exuding something perverse and putrefied.

"Your strategy isn't doing you any favors. As far as I'm concerned, it's not even a threat."

Carmentxu spoke in earnest. My strategy might make her dreadfully uncomfortable, but, when you came down to it, as I said, I was trying to break off my relationship with the group. That desire was rooted in the stabilizing effects of my medication, and there was no way I could satisfy it without external assistance. I would never have dared to say I was no longer going to work for them. Cowardice was a major element in my life: I'd never had the courage to leave any of my lovers, nor could I throw Susana out, although I told myself I could, that as soon as I was earning as much as before, I'd give up the apartment in Aluche and return to Tirso to quietly observe the street, the movements of the people who came and went in the early hours, the glow of headlights in the morning traffic, the flowers, and all those unoriginal neighborhood squares with the bars, and the stores, and the buildings of a city that was not made of rubble, but was solid, however much that solidity might no longer exist. I was filled with an aggravated optimism, and in that state I saw myself returning to a place I'd like to live in, precisely due to my boss believing she could manage without my services. There was absolutely no sense in it.

Carmentxu went on, and now she wasn't just referring to me, but to a general level of stupidity and ineptitude on the part of the whole workforce.

"You're all behaving as if you want revenge instead of trying to negotiate something. But why should I expect it to be any different when you act like adolescents on a daily basis?" she said.

She hesitated for a moment, perhaps expecting some reply, a reply that would have been like squishing a fly in my hands, and then she continued,

"For months I've been thinking about something that happened to me over the last Christmas holiday. On New Year's Eve, I was left stranded at Charles de Gaulle Airport because my flight was overbooked. The other passengers and I decided to complain to Air France, as the only solution they initially offered was spending the night in a hotel in Roissy, near the terminal. A member of the ground staff immediately arrived to say they would find us places on other flights. Before that, when we thought we'd have to stay in Paris, some of the passengers complained more loudly than others, and suggested we should take concerted action. Then, when it was announced they would get us onto other planes as seats became available, those people who'd encouraged the others to complain began jostling their way to the front of the line every time someone from Air France appeared. I remember two of those passengers: a man in his late forties and an Erasmus student who was trying to get home to celebrate her birthday. It was no surprise that those who had been most vocal were rushing to the airline counters to get a seat, and, what's more, there was no need for ridiculous acts of altruism. What was unexpected though, and what I found repugnant, was that when they said we would have to sort out the allocation of seats among ourselves, the ringleaders behaved as if they had never played that role. The Erasmus student leaned on the counter and plaintively tried to convince the rest of the travelers how important it was for her to get home that night, because absolutely all her family and friends were waiting to celebrate her birthday, and the drinks had already been bought, and some of the food was perishable. The way she told it, they'd spent the last thirty-six hours waiting for her with the beers, Fantas, and wine already poured, and the towers of sandwiches covered with napkins were beginning to smell bad. It was New Year's Eve; the other passengers most likely also had parties to attend, and their own plans for the night, but no one else insisted so strongly. Beside her, the man who had led the protest said nothing, just watched her and occasionally smiled. When the airline employee appeared for the third time, this man elbowed the Erasmus student to one side and gave his own name. He was determined to be at the head of the line. The Erasmus student looked to be on the verge of tears and hysteria, and shouted her name to the employee as well. I went on watching the man; not only had he led the protests, but I liked the look of him. I'll confess, the prospect of spending a night in a hotel on the outskirts of Paris, with the Tour Pleyel in the distance, the lights of the city, the traffic on the highway, drinking a glass of wine with that guy, and then taking him to bed, was appealing. And it was within the realm of possibility: during the time we thought we'd have to check into a hotel, we'd been giving each other suggestive looks. I'm always imagining that sort of situation, but usually do nothing about it, so fantasizing about a fuck with the spontaneous leader of a revolt by Air France passengers was no big deal. What's more, I love it when breaches open up, and when things take an unexpected turn. I like it when the car breaks down halfway to my destination, and I have to spend the night in some small town I'd never have even considered stopping in otherwise, or when there's a power outage—though that hasn't happened for a long time—and the air is filled with the scent of candles and camping-stove fuel. I like lazing around in a blackout, spending two, four, six hours, a whole day, not doing any of the things I'd planned; it's when I'm closest to the keenness of the senses I had when I was younger. Nevertheless, the promise of that short period, with the passengers fighting like cats and dogs among themselves, came to nothing. I got ready to start shouting, but when I found myself in the middle of that jostling and the justifications muttered through gritted teeth, I moved away from the crowd and sat on the floor. I decided not to argue with anyone. And I was also trying to ensure the man I'd been thinking of spending the night with would feel guilty. Maybe it was just spite, but when I saw the despicable way he'd managed to get to the head of the line, I was certain I didn't want to sleep with him after all. He glanced at me a couple of times, not because he was still interested in a game of seduction that would no longer end in sex and easy confidences, but because of my attempt to shame him, to let him know I was disgusted by his predatory tactics, his thinly disguised violence. Just as I was disgusted by the pushing and shoving of the other passengers—the triumphant looks of the elderly women greedily grabbing cans of Coca-Cola and sandwiches without being either hungry or thirsty, but just to feel they had gotten something over on the company that had left them stranded on the ground. I didn't think I was any different than them, because in the end I was there taking my revenge, or trying to, and the joys of that revenge were personal and mean. Except for going to the restroom and buying a snack, I didn't leave my place on the floor until all the other passengers had been allocated seats; then I went up to the counter, and was informed there were no more flights to Madrid that night. I was taken to a tacky luxury hotel with a glass-ceilinged lobby in the form of a pyramid, on which fell a light rain that never reached the potted palms by the reception desk. From outside, the palms looked plastic. For a moment, I imagined they must have been brought from Algeria by people coming to visit their poor relations in Seine-et-Marne. That was a completely illogical fantasy because the hotel wasn't even part of an Arab chain, and rich Arabs are unlikely to have poor relations living on the outskirts of Paris. It was midnight when I got there; nothing was open, and I had to make do with the contents of the minibar in my room. Hotels like that are full of businessmen, all asleep and snoring at that hour. I finished off the small bottles of liquor in the fridge, watched TV, and slept for a few hours until it was time to get up; I took a couple of laps around the block to wake myself up, but felt even more stupid than the day before.

"The dawn sun had already seeped into a clear sky like a gleaming white stone, more appropriate for the southern Mediterranean than northern France, and was sparkling on the avenues and beltways. The drizzle was turning to snow; for an instant it was like being in an icy Marrakesh. Years before, I'd spent Christmas in Fez and Chefchaouen, and I remembered the dirty snow on the outskirts of some of the cities I passed through on the bus. Roissy was vaguely similar; it was a landscape that would never be like Madrid, for nothing more than a simple matter of light. The plateau is different, there are no nuances, it's as if the atmosphere plummets down, and the clouds tip out their contents. There's something too high, too rugged, too dry; if you drive out of Madrid, east along the A-3, you don't see anything but a smattering of rocky outcrops covered in black bushes, not dissimilar to giant fungi. They're like a plague of dead locusts on the ground. It's ugly scenery, but I like it. My father's family comes from Fuentidueña de Tajo, about forty-five minutes from the capital, and I spent part of my childhood there, in the middle of the high plain. The tourists don't come that far. Sometimes, when I go there to visit, I turn off the highway and drive along some back road. And the truth is, except for the hills, except for those strange volcano-like mounds rising steeply from the flatness, it's La Mancha, the flat earth with its horizon suggesting a void; and when I say void, not emptiness, I mean something vast. I've always believed a void is full of shapeless things. No one's interested in constructing residential districts there; anyone who's tried has failed, because the brick-making industry is in decline, but you won't see any ecologists fighting for the survival of the black scrub. An environment like that isn't even a beautiful wasteland. What the fungus makes you think of is having left behind a Dantesque slag heap. When I was a teenager, and came back with my parents from trips to the beach, the first traffic jams started around where the fungus bushes grew, and it never occurred to me to think of that landscape as a single entity. I always viewed it as if it were an adjunct to something else, a sign of a nearby suburb putting out roots to suck up the water and minerals of the plain. I've always turned my back on the mountains; my family left Fuentidueña for Palomeras when I was eleven, and our apartment faced a park; I went to state schools, and didn't begin to look at the posh mountain suburbs until I was studying philosophy in Madrid. We were only able to go spend a couple of weeks at the beach in the summer because my father had bought into a time-share apartment complex, although sometimes we went north to the Basque Country, to my mother's hometown. As there were six of us girls, and only one salary coming in, we could barely make ends meet. I'm the youngest; before I began earning money when I was eighteen, I'd never had any new clothes, not even for my birthday. Nowadays, I wonder if the liking of breaches I mentioned before has something to do with the years I spent in a state of siege, trapped by lack of money. Breaches make it possible to forget my former caution.

"I didn't mean to go on like this. I just wanted to say you reminded me of the episode with the plane. If they sack me, I'm going to try my luck for a while outside Spain, outside any enclosed space, far away from books. This isn't the way to be in books. I spend the whole day calculating profits, designing publicity campaigns, and writing articles for literary blogs that are a waste of time because no one can get enough followers, and people are reading less and less. I want to forget it all, and go back to the classics, be in Modena or Berlin, and spend the mornings poking around narrow backstreets, the afternoons in cafés, and then go to a movie in the evening. I'd live that way until my money ran out. It's not a particularly audacious plan, though I do feel a little alarmed every time I check my bank balance. I'm always being told I was born under a lucky star; maybe that's why I can fantasize about drifting aimlessly from one city to another until I'm broke."

Carmentxu dipped a finger into her cold coffee and then sucked it; it was one of her habitual gestures, a perhaps childhood tic she had never grown out of; at times we would giggle at her unintentionally amusing act, and then she felt good about our noticing, but she didn't bother to take it any further. She gave me a look of wary truce, and I had the impression she wasn't keeping a watchful eye on me, but on herself. Her speculative strolls through Cádiz or Naples might have reached other, more skeptical ears; but I was just imagining scenes of foreign places, with my boss in them, and didn't know what to say to her. I'd always thought she was between forty-five and fifty, but wasn't sure. She was a mature woman, and would probably soon be suffering heart problems due to smoking, and her alcohol and coffee intake. She used to wear designer clothes by Serrano and Velásquez to counterbalance a waist like a tub and a double chin suspended over her exquisite necklaces with good taste and an occasional touch of ostentation that was never vulgar. She walked with her back straight and a slight swing of the hips, and had a penchant for high boots and pantyhose with arabesque designs. And she had that sexy-autonomous-region-president look, the sort of sexiness that comes from a lot of discreet power, and I always thought she wore too many variants of long earrings for the tough life of an editor bent all day over manuscripts, though the latter thought is just prejudice on my part. I'd already spent several years viewing that just-a-manager air some editors adopt, and in fact, that's what they mostly are. Another of my prejudices was that no one in the book trade is capable of voting for a right-wing political party; it was an innate vision that was struggling for survival because, despite all, there was a certain consolation in believing it. And it was quite likely no one in the company would vote for a party on the right, even if they did subscribe to a sort of fashionable left that got higher class the more floors you ascended, or sometimes even cooler. The people of my generation with permanent posts were the nephews, nieces, and grandchildren of the founders of the publishing group, educated in exclusive schools with master's degrees in business administration; the one's of my generation in the upper echelons looked down on the writers and ordinary workers like me from the heights of their pride in their designer clothes, and tans, and gym-molded glutes. They sometimes suffered from mild intellectual inferiority complexes, because they had landed in their jobs having read only the absolute minimum—and that with gritted teeth—and a somewhat tardy realization that a solid understanding of the humanities is an element of distinction that takes more than a short course to acquire. They were terrified to discover this; at their private colleges, and during their graduate studies, they had rubbed shoulders with the children of wealthy businessmen who knew nothing about the cultural world, and all that was required of them to be accepted was to get adequate grades, be good-looking, and have the right sort of car. Many of them were aware that they would always be like someone who learned a musical instrument late in life, struggling to attain minor virtuosity, because they don't have the talent to create something from a difficult situation. The most resentful of them looked at you with hatred and tried to humiliate you.

My boss continued her speech, and the longer she talked, the stronger my urge was to say something, to participate in that revelation about herself, which was unique, not because she'd never before opened up in that way, but because she'd never done so with me. When I worked in the office, I'd heard her chatting away for hours to certain employees, or some of the authors. She used to speak naturally, never noticing just how long the other had been silent. I'd been silent for so long there was every possibility Carmentxu would just go on talking until her larynx gave up the ghost. The manuscript of the widow of the postwar writer lay on her desk, and I tried putting it in my bag to see if this would dissuade Carmentxu from continuing her monologue; luckily, her cell phone rang, and I took advantage of the break to say I was going. She seemed relieved. I got to my feet as she was ending the call and waved goodbye.

14

I set the widow's book aside for a day, made a rough draft of Carmentxu's monologue, then concentrated on making it more readable for my psychiatrist. My idea was that, in a literary sense, all my working-life woes were set down there. I eventually thought better of it, and began writing the letter he had asked me for. The "what you put into it, what you get back, what you hope for, and how you organize your time" he'd advised me to refer to in the letter was rattling about in my head, and I was unsure whether to start writing in a practical way, almost in the style of a petition:

> SUBJECT: Self-imposed labor exploitation
> REQUEST: Blahblahblah.

or alternatively to write a formal letter, answering the questions without clarification. My first attempt went like this:

Dear Dr. ———,

I am grateful that you have not simply prescribed
me pills as—so I am told—the majority of psychi-
atrists do. With reference to the topics you have
asked about, I find it hard to reply without rage, or
to give precise quantities, or whatever it is you feel
to be the object of the exercise. As you know, my
mind is occupied by what seems a limitless fog.
For a few months, my impression has been that
what I put into my work is my fog, and after that
something like a degree of efficiency. But I'll try to
express myself as clearly as possible, and stick to
what might form part of a therapy session if you
eventually decide to refer me to a psychologist,
which is what I think I need. Since I've been taking the pills, and so can sleep at night, what I put
in is five working hours in the morning, which I
only partially utilize because I open several newspaper websites, and Facebook, and blogs, and also
look at photographs on Google. All this—that is
to say, checking out what has become of my former classmates, or people I met one summer and
have never seen again—gives me a great deal of
amusement. I don't do it every day, but when I
do I can spend hours trawling through life stories
that never say anything relevant and, to be honest,
I'm not really interested in.

I stopped the first draft of my letter there. It felt too nice,
too ordinary. What was it to the psychiatrist if I was

wasting time? I decided on a dossier format:

What do you put in? Five hours in the morning with too many interruptions. Bored dedication. I occasionally learn something if the book is a long essay. I find satisfaction in a job well done. But then I remember I'm not fairly paid, and do it less well. In the afternoons I don't usually manage more than four hours, unless I have a deadline. But I sit in front of the computer screen until nine, or ten, or even later. I allow myself to waste a lot of time because it helps fill the whole day, and then I don't get anxious. And I've gotten used to it. I've got nothing better to do.

What do you get back? They owe me for fifteen pieces of work. I'm only paid for the urgent books. I'm given any sort of text at all to proofread. I don't know how much longer they are going to need my services. As I'm not fully contracted, they don't feel any need to offer me explanations. The tax office treats me as if I were a large company, when in fact I'm nothing more than the independent contractor of a large publishing group that will never formally employ me again.

What do you hope for? I'm a skeptic, and I expect very little. I'd like to be paid what I'm owed; I'd like my proofreading rate to be increased, and not to be overloaded with work. I'd like my working hours (which are long, even when I do waste time) to give me enough to pay for a downtown apartment, without having to share, to have a month's vacation, to have a life without worries, and not to have to go running to my father whenever I break the lenses in my glasses. I suppose I should be enterprising, as the booklets from the courses for freelancers I've studied suggest, but I'm too depressed and worn out right now.

How do you organize your time? As must be obvious, extremely badly.

The dossier option seemed satisfactory, and when I came out of my bedroom I found Susana waiting for me, the teapot in hand. It occurred to me that it was the first time I hadn't heard her coming in and moving around the apartment, and I considered that a triumph of the pills, or my newfound ability to concentrate on my own problems.

15

Having achieved a more organized daily schedule and control, or something resembling it, over my fears, I was able to
recommence my nocturnal walks. I would set out, buoyed
by the anti-reuptake properties of the high doses of sero-
tonin and noradrenalin I'd been prescribed. The side effects
were still a little weird, since unlike Germán, who got used
to them and stabilized *on the medication*, I was completely
aware throughout the whole day that I was taking several
drugs, which had a variety of missions within my nervous
system, and thus my head, and which cloaked—or perhaps
simply lulled—a sort of aporia. I didn't abandon my basic
mistrust, or stop observing myself from a watchtower, as
if a neural zone in my mind had achieved a state of Zen
that was fighting off some other, more hysterically resistant
flank. It didn't make me nervous; I was bordering on a state
of mild stupor. The psychiatrist had told me the toxins never
had the same effect on any two individuals; people reacted

quite differently, and some never became accustomed to them, never *functioned normally* on the medication. That "never" sounded to me as though I was going to spend the rest of my life drugged up in order to *function normally on the medication.*

I had no desire to return to the places I'd frequented during the winter and spring, places that now reminded me of the monster. I eschewed Eugenia de Montijo, the wasteland where the prison had stood, and Carabanchel in general, and began heading for the adjoining neighborhood of Usera. That involved a bus journey, but I didn't mind. Then I would return to the outskirts of the city from the Doce de Octubre metro station, which meant cutting my walks pretty short; the last train left at 11:47, and at 12:04 I'd be at Aluche station. So much punctuality in what had formerly been a chaotic life allowed me to recreate myself, as if the train schedule was coupled to my will in an impression of being in charge. In Usera, I was at first interested in the Chinatown, where everything stayed open very late, although it wasn't the stores that caught my attention as much as the gentle bustle around them. I also noticed the restaurants. If the menu included rice noodles with crab, I would go in. Then I'd meander around the commercial streets and explore, as was my habit, the residential areas in the direction of Doce de Octubre. Some neighborhoods adjoining Almendrales had the appearance of being survivors of a long-past period. The buildings whose façades had been renovated seemed to be covered in a layer of thin paper, and those with the brick still on view looked like they were still in the process of construction. The council can't have put much money into giving those buildings face-lifts over the last forty years; the glassed-in balconies were crammed with bikes, fans, chairs, bags, and pillowcases perhaps containing macramé curtains or decapitated Playmobil figures, so it was as if each floor was inhabited by three generations of a single family. The silence, on the other hand, suggested unoccupied buildings about to be torn down. When I turned onto one of those streets on another occasion, I saw cables strung from some of the balconies to streetlights, stealing electricity. It was only a few, of course, but that didn't stop me from returning to the unlikely conviction that there were underground movements capable of modifying my mental vision of the city, and also the conception of it I read in newspapers, or saw on television and the Internet. This pretty vague conviction—or perhaps, better, off-track intuition—made me uneasy. If accurate, it was equivalent to discovering we were Martians, someone's dream, or a computer program in which the rules changed from day to day. But then the Romanies and homeless families had been occupying the city's empty buildings for decades, and since the increase in immigration, many dwellings on the outskirts had been broken into. I'd heard stories of family members being unable to come to an agreement about what to do with their inheritance, of empty properties perched on the slopes on either side of the railroad tracks, or boxed in between new buildings when, for complex legal reasons, they could not be expropriated. The heirs allowed homeless families to live in the disputed buildings for the cost of maintenance. At one time I'd taken an interest in uncovering such phenomena, and used to prowl the streets where the aged houses seemed to be fresh and flourishing, but that was all I'd been able to confirm.

16

"Janssen and I have decided to have a baby," my roommate announced.

"Oh," I replied.

Susana frowned; I guess she expected me to say something more.

"I know you're thinking I'm too old to have children," she continued.

"I haven't had time to think anything," I countered.

"Prejudices don't need thinking out," she retorted.

"My mind was on something else. If you want to know my opinion, what you've just said is nothing more than your own view of yourself. But I am wondering if you're going to get back together with Janssen in Utrecht, or if he's coming here."

"You want to know if I'm planning to leave the apartment."

"No, that didn't occur to me."

"I can't say anything until I get pregnant."

"But it must at least mean you two have come to some kind of an understanding."

"We haven't come to any understanding. But we get along well together, and we want to do it."

Susana brought me a cup of rooibos tea in one of the cups with a cow design I cart from apartment to apartment. I'd bought them one of the summers I spent in small Irish towns, learning English with a view to my promising future. I stayed with families where the women had the same pale complexion as Susana, and her blue eyes, although none of them were either tall or corpulent. All I remember about Ireland is the coastal scenery between Greystones and Bray, and the afternoon some friends and I broke a window of a tumbledown empty house and scrambled in. There were no bats, no rat skeletons, just columns made of packs of A4 paper. The packs were old, the paper yellowing; we took as many as we could carry and scattered the sheets of paper along the beach. I haven't been back to Ireland since that summer.

"Well, cheer up. I don't know what else to say to you."

"You don't have to say anything."

"How are your maps coming along?"

"Almost finished. Do you want to see them?"

She didn't wait for me to answer, but got to her feet, went to her room, and returned with a bulging folder. I hadn't realized she'd put so much work into the project. She laid out the first four maps, which seemed to me both encrypted and exhausting, with their Madrid buildings all jumbled and reassembled with apparently machine-like precision. I recalled what Susana had told me about the difference between manually pasting minute images and making the maps using a computer program.

"I'm not sure I could recognize Madrid without a magnifying glass."

"Me neither. That's why I did a few maps that are just of neighborhoods. See if you can guess which ones."

Susana rummaged among the maps and laid out another four, completely covering the table. I inspected them carefully. If I'd seen them hanging on the wall of a gallery, I would have gotten a whiff of a Spanish city, but couldn't have put forward many hypotheses about them.

"That tower with the clock," I said, "is it Puerta del Sol?"

"No, it's the tower in Plaza Fortuna."

I examined the other maps with equal care; it was even more difficult to recognize anything. Susana appeared to have excluded the most obvious landmarks, such as the Gran Vía building with the huge Schweppes advertisement, or La Cibeles. Or perhaps I just couldn't locate them.

"Can I see them all?" I asked.

"Of course you can," she responded in a tone that indicated she was flattered.

"You should try to get an exhibition in some gallery."

Susana exuded even greater satisfaction, and walked back and forth in front of the window, I guess fantasizing about exhibiting her work in a gallery, while I looked at the other maps. I couldn't identify any specific neighborhood, although it was obvious which ones were probably in the center, and which beyond the M-30. The latter reminded me of my walks, not because I had a clear image of the city, but due to the chaos. I would have liked to buy those maps from her, but could see how excited she was and didn't want to water down her upbeat mood with a stingy offer. My wallet wouldn't stretch to anything better.

"Is it the first time you've done such a systematic collection of work?"

"You know I spend my days doing this sort of stuff," she replied. "I make things, keep them for a while, and then burn them or trash them. I don't want to live with bits of paper everywhere. What I actually want is to do something with the notes I've been making, and the photographs."

"Wouldn't it be better to focus on what you do well?" I responded, and immediately regretted my words. I'd just suggested she didn't know how to write, and her photographs weren't interesting. Susana was unperturbed.

"Perhaps," she said. "I like doing the maps, but I'm so used to them, I can't see if they are good or not. Do you know anyone who could help out?"

Susana had pronounced that question with a sort of afflicted eagerness, as if something was coming to an end, and she suspected the future was not going to turn out well. I shared that feeling. I had no idea why I should have a hunch about something that didn't concern me, but neither did I care. I felt like a dog barking as it freed itself from its leash to run for the mountains the night before a tsunami.

"We can ask around. It won't be so hard to at least get people to listen to you," I said.

"What's your plan?"

"Well, to go around the galleries…asking."

"Right," said Susana sarcastically.

Her tone exasperated me in a way that was quite different from my usual reaction: boredom or rudeness. She seemed like a spoiled child who expected someone else to solve all her problems.

"I often go for long walks," I said nevertheless, and in addition to my foreboding and exasperation, I noted a level of dread: the vision of the guys from the truck—the sheets of sharp-edged cardboard with which they beat the darkness—flitted through my mind. "I can set out earlier, and we can visit galleries together. Bring your maps, and show them around."

"OK," was Susana's response.

I was surprised she would give way so easily, and equally astonished when she opened her HP Mini to make a list of galleries we could visit. I retreated to my room, oppressed by the possible fate of the maps of the dismantled city. My earlier distress was now mingling with this sense of foreboding until they fused into a single entity. I was afraid of finding a link between the cardboard collectors and Susana's map project. Even worse, I could see a direct and clear connection between the two. But what did that evidence reveal? On the evening set aside for visiting the galleries, Susana arrived home from work early, took all the maps from her folder, and spent quite a long time questioning me about their suitability.

"Shall we go?" I asked after about an hour spent making choices, and not because I had any desire to tour galleries; I too had begun to examine the maps obsessively.

While looking at them, and responding to my roommate's questions about which were best, I'd begun to think that the compositions were not innocent, and hadn't sprung from Susana's head, but were replicating something present in the environment. When we'd boarded the metro, she took the maps from the folder again to scrutinize them, and it seemed to me they melded with the surrounding air. We got off at Alonso Martínez and opened up our street plan. Susana had marked out a route in dots of pink highlighter pen. With a touch of distaste, I scanned the sturdy, slightly soiled elegance of the buildings in this neighborhood I'd always wanted to live in. The first gallery, a small, and to me comforting space, had contemporary versions of still lifes with packages of donuts and the remains of French fries scattered around perfect partridges and skulls.

"Hi," said Susana to a young man. "Are you the gallery owner?"

"No, I manage the place."

"And the owner? When will he be in?"

"He's a she. Her name's Laura Díaz. What did you want?"

"To show her what I do."

"You can leave your CV and photocopies of your work."

"Ah, I hadn't thought of that," said Susana.

We went back onto the street without saying another word, and walked around for a few minutes, slightly disoriented. An embittered expression was settling on Susana's finely lined face. While I repented having encouraged her to take part in a sort of *Spain's Got Talent*, I was grateful for that brush with reality. We went into a photocopy store.

"I'm not going to leave my CV, that would be absurd. I haven't got one," she said as the machines emitted their rhythmical hum.

We started out again to the same rhythm as the machines, and with a rapidity unusual for either of us, we made our way along Chamberí, Chueca, and a few streets in the Salamanca neighborhood, leaving copies in the galleries on the list. We saw, among other things: an exhibition of photographs apparently representing blood; another of shaven nudes; another with tiny figures of iron or some other metal; the fourth had blurry blobs; the fifth conventional seascapes to hang in apartments; and another had Pop landscapes in oils. I came to no conclusion about the possibility of finding a home for the maps. And neither did Susana. By the end, we were meandering rather than walking; on a couple of occasions my roommate was incapable of crossing the threshold of one of those lively premises, and I had to hand over the copies. None of the gallery owners were present; the managers accepted her work in silence, with routine efficiency and, once or twice, lethargy.

"I'm like one of those people who hand out leaflets you throw in the first trashcan you come across," she said when we arrived at the tenth and last gallery, which was already closed for the evening, and whose manager took Susana's copies with a grumpy expression. "But on the other hand, I'm beginning to think I could do that sort of work too. Those managers are just as bored as I am answering calls."

I could think of no response to that, and didn't even know what tone would satisfy her. She seemed to long for a job that would offer her some level of fulfillment, but was then comforted to discover what she coveted was no better than what she already had. She spent the following days waiting for glorious phone calls that never arrived, and I told her it was normal that they didn't get too excited about the maps at first sight. I managed not to look at them as I spoke.

"It's not that," she replied.

She sat looking pensively at her work, as if she expected to find errors; I couldn't work out what type of error they might contain that hadn't been immediately visible. The quality of the finish of the individual pieces seemed to me unimportant, and I guessed it was the same for Susana. By the end of the week, she no longer even wanted to talk about the maps, for which I was grateful. She went around with a hangdog expression, as if she had actually had an exhibition and it had been the most spectacular flop—confirmation of the uselessness of everything she did, of her very existence. It was time to forget the whole thing. There was no sense in harping on about it, but nevertheless my fear, and that earlier foreboding, the shapeless something that seemed to be the result of my illness, led me to say:

"I think it would be better to rule out the galleries. I'm going to look for bars that have exhibitions. OK?"

Susana answered with a terse affirmative. For the two days it took me to find a bar, she didn't say a single word, although her enormous, taciturn presence filled the living room. She showed no signs of trying to meet Janssen in cyberspace, didn't even switch on her laptop. For my part, I managed not to think. I was like a sleepwalker obeying orders from some part of me I had to silence. There was no way of knowing how she would react when she saw the bar I'd checked out; it was small, on a quiet street, and not the best space for an exhibition, not even by an amateur artist.

I'd stopped in by chance to take a rest, and while it wasn't the typical bar with artsy-fartsy aspirations, it felt ideal for my roommate. I could imagine her sitting at one of the tables with her laptop. When I explained the matter to the owner, he raised no objections, and didn't even request a fee or ask to see Susana's work. His only comments were that a friend of his was doing his PhD on Renaissance cartography, and the exhibition was a great idea. It would have made no difference to him if we'd hung a collection of tablecloths instead of maps. That uncomplicated enthusiasm fit in well with Susana's personality.

It didn't ring true to me that my roommate had given me details about her past that hadn't reached my conscious mind, but were lodged in some region of the brain, giving the impression there was no such thing as coincidence, only causality. When I told her I'd found a bar near Huertas, a bar called Las Meninas, and then immediately added the name of the street, Susana raised her eyebrows, her jaw dropped, and she stayed in that pose for what seemed like minutes, gripped by an astonishment as mute as the really irritating silence that had preceded it.

"What's wrong?" I asked.

"Could you repeat the address?"

I repeated it. She chewed at one of her nails and responded, "That's the bar where I had my dates twenty years ago. It used to be called El Cuatro."

She pronounced those words with atypical naturalness, with none of her usual affected tone.

"If you don't want to have the exhibition there, I can look for someplace else."

I noted that I was nervous, feeling guilty of an unconscious faux pas, as if I'd been hypnotized into putting Susana in a time warp that could possibly destabilize her, make her shatter into shards that would be impossible to remove from her flesh.

"When you said the name of the street, I saw myself phoning the newspapers and giving the address in just that same way, blurting it out," continued Susana.

She sat there in a trance, pulling at her nail until it became painful and she'd extracted blood. The muscles in her face tensed, and that tension hovered for a few seconds over the physical pain of the flesh around her nail, which took advantage of the momentary inattention to tip over into something else. Perhaps it was the same fear that had held her in its grip during those last days, and was now receiving unexpected confirmation.

"I couldn't not want to, even if I wanted to," she continued. "And I'm not going to put you to any further bother. Are the walls still blue?"

"They're pink now."

"Pink is perfect," she said in a flat tone, although her mind was undoubtedly on her maps, about how they would look on that backdrop.

I thought perhaps it wasn't the same bar, and suggested we check it out on Street View. The images we found had been shot on a cloudy day; the interior looked cold through the darkened windows.

"Yes, that's it," said Susana. "Is it run by an old guy named Tobías?"

"The man I spoke to would be in his late forties, and his

name is Pedro. He said he was from Guadalajara."

"It's changed hands then."

"Most likely." I remembered that the man had been wearing a T-shirt with a message I'd read and almost instantly forgotten. I added, "He told me a friend of his was doing a PhD in cartography."

"Really?"

Her head seemed to be still occupied by another matter she didn't reveal to me, and which I don't believe had anything to do with her faith in coincidences, the phone calls that had never come, or the messed-up life within which she was recreating herself. Susana was convinced it was too late, the damage was done, and she wasn't going to make any effort to do a single thing that didn't prove her conviction to be true. But now there was a different intensity to her hopelessness. Something was happening: she was going over things, checking. When I rose to move to the haven of my room, she said:

"I walked past that bar for years, and I still do now that I'm back in Madrid, but I never really thought about it until you mentioned the address. I sometimes dream of its blue walls, and the clientele. Those women with their dentures and fat bellies. I remember some of them used to spend the whole afternoon there. And before they'd even finished their reheated croissant and coffee, they'd be ordering a dish of pickled anchovies. It's never occurred to me to go in there again."

Over the days that followed I neglected my work and helped her to prepare her exhibition. It wasn't a matter of generosity; I simply couldn't think about anything else. We went to the bar on several evenings, and found ourselves among an elderly local fauna fiddling with their decafs and Cola Caos, plus another collection of new-age drop-outs who fit in with the barman's aesthetic. Susana made an effort not to let it get her down. She often interrupted the owner when he was talking about where to hang her work, or how to protect the pieces from the damp in the walls, to say she was going outside to check how the maps looked from the street. I guessed she wasn't checking anything; she was just looking at the bar to torture herself for having been incapable of recognizing it over all those years, despite having passed it, dreamed of it, frequently thought of the time she'd spent there on blind dates. Susana would come back inside looking shocked, and drink a couple of vermouths. I grew concerned she'd suffer another psychotic episode. Nothing of the sort happened; her only suffering was a proud, unspoken sadness.

"Anyone could show their dumb stuff here. It doesn't mean my work's any good," she said not long before the opening.

When the day arrived, she changed her shift, and spent the whole morning trying out clothes and hairstyles, all strange and severe. I thought: tonight she really is going to cheat on Janssen. I don't know why I thought that; from the time she'd started planning the exhibition, my roommate had no time for anything but the maps. When I asked if Janssen would be coming to the opening, she said, "I used to make collages when I lived in Utrecht, and I threw art parties, but always at home. Janssen's already had enough of my work." Her formidable, muscular rump ended up crammed into some sort of dark crimson velvet riding pants, over which she wore a white shirt, buttoned to the neck and very close fitting around the bust. From the side, she looked like a letter *Z* with a head and legs.

We arrived at the bar early that evening. I helped Susana hang the maps and then she had a beer, and I had a nonalcoholic one because the psychiatrist had told me not to drink. My roommate had gone back to being excited, eager to get started; I wondered what hopes she had for the exhibition. The most modest would perhaps be to sell her maps, earn a little extra money, or even make a living from her work in minor art circles, like someone who sells crafts. She might also be toying with the scenario of some relevant patron coming into the bar and noticing her maps, or even her obsession with miniature clippings; someone who would understand every single thing about that passion. I couldn't imagine what it must mean to compose those detailed collages, only to then destroy them when they began to occupy too much space, but there was a radical difference between burning them in a park and being aware of their worth. Maybe Susana's only ambition was to please her friends, but even if her faith in her failure was as strong as ever, this time she'd taken a step further, and must have other aspirations. Her firmly held beliefs had been shaken. "I couldn't not want to, even if I wanted to," she'd said, and that affirmation was more important than she thought. Susana's hopes had nothing to do with triumph or her maps; she wanted—twenty years after her first visit to that place—the location of her madness to be now the location of her art. I'd swear she was clinging to that invisible thread. New—or not so new—hopes blossomed, but they were not destroyed by failure. And those hopes were not based on a return to the past, but on a suspension of time.

Just before the event was due to begin, Susana started running her hand over her laptop. I'd learned to read some of her gestures; she stroked the computer when she was savoring the moments before an idea became reality. Then she asked Pedro for permission to record the event. After going from map to map with her laptop, she set it down pointing toward the door with the camera still on. When she'd checked no one was going to be left headless, she plugged the laptop into the mains: the guests would be able to witness their own arrival.

"The quality won't be very good," said the owner, but Susana wasn't worried about it being *good*; she wasn't bothered if the result was unsatisfactory.

What was important was taking an idea and observing it unfold.

Before starting the recording, while she was talking to the owner and me, Susana remembered an Argentinian movie. Pedro had asked if her family was coming, to which she replied, "I prefer not to talk about my family."

"A good family is a distant family," he platitudinized so as not to disagree with the artist.

Susana smiled, and I thought she was going to start flirting with him; he was staring at her breasts with barely concealed rapture. But her smile had its source in Argentinian cinema:

"There's a movie by Lucrecia Martel called *The Swamp*," she told us, "where the only free people are the children.

They play, feel each other up, spy, and the adults go on doing their own stuff, away from the orgy. The camera is set to give a child's-eye view. So you see everything from the height of an infant."

The owner and I had waited for her to add something more, but Susana had just taken out her HP Mini, pressed the *on* button, and then had come the recording of the maps and placing the computer on a chair, in imitation of the gaze of a very quiet child watching the adults arrive. The fear had completely disappeared from her face. Perhaps she was grasping the invisible thread for the first time. Susana liked to experiment with what she'd learned, liked to see what it would spark off; it gave her a sense of importance. But that need made her original in a way that could only give rise to mockery.

Pedro didn't get the relationship between the movie and Susana's idea. The elderly locals who had been in the bar all afternoon gathered around to see what was going on. Susana's acquaintances began to arrive in groups. There were no close friends, no one who would be the object of in-on-the-secret glances. It occurred to me that my roommate didn't have close friends because she didn't want them. Her acquaintances, all people in their forties and fifties, stood at a distance, talking among themselves with an air of belonging to another era. Susana went to chat with them, gave them a tour of the maps, and looked toward the door as if expecting someone who had to be there, who must be about to cross the threshold. The atmosphere on the street was warm and welcoming. There were very few stores. The miniature anarchy that was the overriding element of Susana's

maps was disturbing. Pedro had laid out five Spanish om-
elets and six bottles of wine on a couple of tables. Between
our combined acquaintances, and a few drop-ins, there were
about thirty people peering at the work. Toward the culmi-
nation of the evening, Susana began to squawk "Thank you"
in her disagreeable voice. I thought she was afraid of the
people who were observing the maps too closely, the ones
who went right up to the glass to study the composition. As
my roommate tended to eat when she was agitated, there
wasn't a moment when she didn't have a piece of omelet or
bread in her mouth. When those ran out, she began down-
ing glasses of wine, although she did keep up a polite front
until the guests began to drift away into the cool night. She
looked at the door again, and seemed to be still waiting.
Perhaps she was expecting the dwarf I'd christened Fabio
in my text about her unhinged phase. She sat down at the
table that, she'd claimed, was in the same location as the one
where she'd met the men and women who'd answered her
ads twenty years before.

"This is like *Peter's Friends*," she said, and then asked
Pedro if she'd sold anything.

"No," he replied.

I avoided her eyes; not even I had bought anything,
despite the low prices. But I had an excuse, I told myself
miserably.

"When I take down the exhibition, I'll give all the maps
to you," Susana suddenly informed me.

I didn't have the courage to mutter so much as a
"There's no need," or a "Thanks." I didn't want the maps;
the vision of myself in the apartment in Aluche with thirty

arrangements of Madrid on the walls was horrifying.

"I need to walk," she said.

"Me too."

The following day I had to be up early to work all out on the widow of the postwar writer's Parkensonian handwriting. But I wanted to put off that task as long as possible. I wanted to do things less well.

We never actually made a decision to return to the apartment on foot, and it was only after some time that we began to say, "We're over halfway now." We'd crossed the Toledo Bridge, and the recently interred M-30, and were climbing up toward Aluche like two shadows, or two dancing insects. It was early morning; the sanitation workers who swept and washed the downtown streets were as usual nowhere to be seen on the south side of the city, and the dust and hard asphalt were the only things to impinge on the senses. We were thirsty, but once beyond Calle General Ricardos nothing was open. Not even the Chinese restaurants, the bars, or the Dominican nightclubs. Just silence, and the occasional car. Everything was much as usual, yet what lay before my eyes didn't seem like the city I saw every day; it was as if one of Susana's maps had been surreptitiously populated, and now the city was revealing itself as other, was beginning to make sense. I couldn't have put my finger on exactly what that otherness was, but it was clearly there—growing and out to get me. I was terrified we would come across the guys from the truck. While logic told me that they must have finished combing the neighborhood by this hour, and now be on the prowl downtown, taking advantage of the scant police presence, that line of reasoning was no help because everything was following different laws. When I glanced at Susana, my concern dissipated a little; she was unaware of the strangeness we were making our way through. To my eyes, she looked defeated and drunk, and her head seemed to be occupied by a buzzing that made her walk on resolutely, muttering the odd angry phrase. This suited me fine; I needed to get home as soon as possible, or get anywhere that would return my perception of things to the comfortable niche of my everyday madness. I was thinking that Susana and I would always walk that same way, even if we were taking a stroll along the Gran Vía at seven in the evening; I was thinking we'd never spent so much time together outside the apartment, and that it was astonishing how little resistance I put up to finding Susana so like myself, with the same gait that didn't hide the anxiety to reach those trees as soon as physically possible, and then that fuchsia-colored car in the distance, and then that collection of buildings I'd always assumed to be a retirement home, but was in fact a conservatory. And next I thought that if I'd just exhibited something—drawings or a collection of pressed orchids—I'd have felt as nervous as her; I'd have spent the whole evening with my mouth full of omelet and bread and wine, needing to walk afterward to clear my head. Or to lose myself. Or even to find myself in something similar to what I was now experiencing.

When we reached Eugenia de Montijo, where the prison had been demolished the previous winter, I ground to a halt. I was almost bursting with the need to tell Susana about my obsession, and also to ask her where she'd gotten the idea of making different cities on the same grid. What I really wanted to ask was if she'd seen those cities; I wanted her to notice my jitteriness, to look at me, but she just stared into the now empty space, her nose twitching, sniffing out nonexistent scents.

"That's where the prison used to be," was all I managed to say.

"I know. My father served time there. I didn't know it had been torn down."

"It was a few months ago."

"Ah," replied Susana, but added nothing about why her father had been in prison.

And I didn't press her, because that wasn't what I wanted to talk about. If I hadn't been frozen with anxiety, I'd have shrugged my shoulders. I guessed her father had been a political prisoner in the late Franco era, since it didn't seem likely that she came from a family with a criminal background. And then I thought that maybe he'd killed her mother, or one of her sisters, or that he'd raped Susana, with everyone turning a blind eye, which might explain her history of psychosis and the fact that she now had no communication with her family. All those suppositions sped across my field of vision; I wanted to waft them away to get a clearer view of the park, and of the wasteland through the barbed-wire fence; I wanted to return them to the tranquility of their place in my memory. When we were leaving the park, we heard the sound of an engine. It wasn't a car, but some larger vehicle—without looking in the direction of the sound, I knew it was the cardboard collectors' truck. I gave a stifled wail, and told Susana we needed to turn back, not to make any noise. We sat on a bench; my roommate seemed tense, and I didn't know how to tell her about her maps and the city, because it felt like none of that was translatable into language, that I was unable to speak it because I didn't know what it was I had to tell. From that distance, I couldn't be sure if it was the Romany truck; all that was visible were five human forms scavenging in the dumpsters. I noted something pass quickly in front of me; it could have been a leaf falling from the tree we were sitting under, or an insect, as I felt no impact when it touched my skin.

"Frightened?" Susana asked, and I saw she was smiling at me in a way that was somehow complicit and malign.

"Who the hell are you?" I asked in turn.

I got to my feet, and would have started to run if it hadn't been for the five figures gathered on the edge of the park, now looking toward us with the stillness of ghosts.

Continuing to smile, she said, "Are you crazy, or what? Sit down, please."

The five figures dissolved, and Susana told me the plot of an old movie set in a version of Madrid, where there was a secret subterranean fortress in which seven hunchbacks killed people. According to Susana, the movie didn't reveal why the hunchbacks did it. It was, she added, a comedy.

We both stood up, and Susana announced, "I'm going to show you a hermitage, and then we'll make our way back along a path."

I knew the hermitage: a thirteenth-century building across from the prison, next to the Cementerio Paroquial de Carabanchel Bajo.

"There used to be a gravedigger's house here. But then someone decided it spoiled the view of the historical monument, and had it demolished," said Susana with a cackle.

It was the first time I'd stopped to take a closer look at the hermitage. I tried to laugh, but still didn't understand what was going on. I didn't want to leave the park; I was too scared to go anywhere without Susana.

The hole in the fence I'd sneaked through during the winter months—possibly the work of the Romanies—had been repaired. The path between the cemetery and the wasteland appeared to lead into open countryside or orchards, although common sense told me it could only be something more urban. I'd never felt the urge to follow that shortcut during my nocturnal incursions into the area, since there was no escape route if I came across some ill-intentioned person. It seemed equally dangerous now, like a tunnel or narrow alley with no other paths leading off it. My knees were trembling and my palms sweating. I was afraid we would run into the group of five figures again; it only needed the addition of Susana and I to make up the cast of hunchbacks in the comedy she had just told me about. We continued on without a word; it was as if we were trapped under a sky that—in contrast with the sudden darkness—was glowing with the reddish orange of light pollution. I had the impression we were walking through the heavens, and what was spread above our heads was the city. There had been no rain for months; our footsteps left a wake of dust. We came to the end of the path without meeting anyone, and Susana became serious again. My face must have been pale; she looked at me with a degree of surprise, but said nothing. When we reached home, and were taking off our shoes, we noticed dozens of tiny insects clinging to the laces; they initially looked like the seeds of some plant, but when we shook them off they tumbled to the floor and disappeared behind the furniture.

"Fleas," said Susana.

I shook my head.

"Fleas would have gone straight for our skin. We'd already be scratching."

I felt dizzy; possibly I'd been hallucinating for the previous hour and a half, but I wasn't sure. Everything was now solid, and dense; I forced myself to think about those tiny bugs, and came to the conclusion they were spiders. They had also reminded me of the ice patterns on our windows in the fall and winter. I went in search of the can of insecticide and sprayed the backs of the chairs in the living room, and the shelves with Susana's books, leaves, and jars of colored salts. She watched her novels and manuals being covered in poison without making any other objection than, "We'll have to wash our hands every time we read something." I agreed, went to my bedroom, and continued spraying insecticide there; then I went out onto what had once been a metal balcony, but was now a tiny, glassed-in area that was rarely used since in winter it was too cold to spend much time there, and in summer you fried. Nevertheless, I stayed there over an hour that night, looking out on the view without knowing what to ask of it. I didn't even notice the distance that separated me from the places I'd have liked to inhabit, and everything smelled toxic, and I only wanted to deal with immediate things: those bugs flitting like tiny dragonflies from our boots to the furniture, and from there to who knows where. The windows of the ersatz balcony were wide open to let out the stench of insect killer. I hadn't said goodnight to Susana, but that didn't matter. Neither had I taken my medication, and that *did* matter, although not enough for me to abandon my observation post over the wasteland where pale yellow hedge mustard grew in spring, and which allowed me a Tetris-scale view of the Palacio Real, the ugly Almudena Cathedral, the dome of the Basílica San Francisco el Grande, the Moncloa transmission tower with its restaurant that no one patronized on the observation deck, the unimpressive buildings of the University City. I went on unconsciously interrogating the cityscape, just as it manifested itself to me from the balcony in some way that was impossible to gauge. From there everything fit in the palm of my hand, extended toward an illusory sky.

17

While I was rewriting the widow's book, Susana received a call from Pedro. A gallery owner had seen the exhibition in the bar, and wanted to talk to her. Susana was incredulous.

I'd spent the morning revising my text about her; I wanted it to offer some form of certainty, some clue that would be followed by a string of others, like the lights of an airport at night, without which the planes cannot land. Her news sent me into new levels of confusion; the moment hadn't yet come to consider whether or not my text was valid, but the desire to get things right was urging me to do so. Was beginning Susana's story with a provocation a serious problem? And when I considered some motives to be more serious than others was I perhaps allowing myself to be carried along by conservative criteria? Was my viewpoint fair, or had I been tendentious? These questions hid another I was incapable of asking myself: Was there any chance that madness was *real*? Susana went to her bedroom to call the art dealer, and when she returned to the living room her face was aglow.

"Apparently, she's really excited about the maps, and would like to show them in her gallery," Susana said.

"What's her name? Is she any good?"

"Olga Romero. And no idea how good she is. According to the guy from the bar, she lives nearby, and noticed the maps because she passes by every morning. Her name sounds familiar, and I might have visited her gallery some time, but that's all I know."

"We could Google her," I said.

"Can I use your computer? Mine takes so long to boot up."

Susana typed in the name, and the search engine swamped us with hits from newspapers and art sites: "Olga Romero, today's most fashionable art dealer"; "The Olga Romero Gallery, where every artist wants to show"; "Olga Romero, savior of the arts." Spanish artists such as Miquel Barceló, José Manuel Broto, Alberto García-Alix, and Ferran García Sevilla had begun their careers in that famous gallery, which also showed works by other artists with international reputations neither Susana or I had heard of.

"I can't believe it," she said, repeating the phrase several times.

This was indeed like a movie script, but for once Susana didn't mention cinema.

"Congratulations," I said insincerely. "What did she say?"

"She wants to see what I've got."

"And how much have you got?" I asked, rather ashamed.

I had never asked her to show me the collages she had made in Utrecht. I'd imagined them to be of no particular value, and thought it was enough to look at her disordered maps of Madrid, even if they did disturb me.

"I don't know if it's a lot or not much, if it's good or bad. I don't know the first thing. What am I going to say when she asks me? That I make *art brut*? That sounds ridiculous."

"Why? And you go to lots of exhibitions. You must know something."

I heard my voice tear apart in a purely mental way; the slow rent sounded in my brain like the ticktock of clocks in commercials.

"Yes, I go to lots of exhibitions, but I don't know how to judge my stuff. I don't have the background. Reading about art bores me. I always pass on the catalogs; I like looking."

I shouldn't have been wasting any more time. I had a deadline for the widow's book. But maybe I could just go to my bedroom, take out my notebook, examine the text about Susana's madness. Calm my doubts. One page, I told myself, just one page will be enough. But then I remembered Fabio, and the dates, and the ghostly voices issuing from the answering machine, and I felt it was no good, out of my reach, or only possible in some terrifying way. The text would be as I remembered it. As if I were Susana. I followed her to her room. Under the bed, in bags, were around twenty files holding individual miniature images and overloaded, ferocious, exhausting compositions. She glanced at them and then passed them to me. I thought that if she asked me to go away, I'd refuse. I couldn't leave the room until I'd *calculated* the significance of it all. It was an unachievable aim.

"Thank goodness I didn't throw it all out," she said. I've still got everything I did over the last two years in Utrecht."

"Haven't you kept anything from earlier?"

"Only the things I didn't have the courage to destroy, because Janssen liked them."

"And haven't you given any away as presents?"

"A few. A Dutch friend told me he liked what I did, but wouldn't want to hang it over his TV. So I stopped giving my collages away. I hate the idea of anyone having to hang something they find disturbing."

"She told you to bring everything, right?"

"Yes, but it seems like too much. I don't think there's anything better than the maps."

"You've just said you don't know how to judge them."

"I have hunches about what I do."

"Take it all," I ordered. "Let her decide. We can call Germán and ask him to give us a lift."

"She offered to come here, but I didn't think the apartment was the right place to show it all."

"It isn't."

"I need to separate the finished maps and collages from the collections of clippings."

"Take the collections too."

Susana looked at me in stupefaction, not understanding my commands. I didn't understand them either.

"When's your appointment?"

"The day after tomorrow."

I spent two more hours in her bedroom, looking at her collages. There was a strong, material smell of glue; something sweet slipping through the air. Then I went out onto the street. I had an overwhelming urge for movement that made me walk as if I knew where I was going. I went as far as Lucero. On my way back, while passing by a block of buildings under repair, I was forced to move into the road. It was then that something thrown from the back of a vehicle turning the corner hit me in the temple. I scarcely had time to get a glimpse of the truck. Not because I didn't look, but when that object hit me I bent my head, the truck disappeared, and I was left with a slight trickle of blood, drops joining together to form a fine line. I couldn't be sure exactly what had wounded me. Nor did I know if it had been thrown on purpose or had detached itself from the back of the truck, as used to happen with the straw loaded onto agricultural vehicles. I looked around for the projectile, found nothing, and so continued walking uphill, guided by instinct, because as usual I didn't know the precise way home, but followed my intuition in relation to diagonals and hills and certain colors, and the general layout of my surroundings profiled in my head as plans of corners, sidewalks—the simple jolt of suddenly coming across a house with a small palm tree opposite a flight of steps winding from one level of ground to another. After a while, when I'd reached an avenue like some kind of empty nocturnal plain, the guys from the truck reappeared, and I heard a few whistles. Then I saw the hand, and what's more, was able to imagine it in its task of scavenging among the boxes to find small triangles with the consistency of wood, even though they might be sheets of paper stuck together, the edge of which struck my face again, this time on the chin. I bent and picked up that cellulose agglomeration; there was no way it could kill anyone. I heard yells, and streamers fell from the truck. On closer inspection, I realized they weren't streamers but rolls of paper from some old fashioned continuous feed printer, with their Braille-like language, their code of tiny holes decorating the asphalt. Was this a game of inoffensive missiles? How did they manage to hit parts of the body that didn't hurt, to leave no trace of the attack? Was I inventing a history of aggressions involving nothing more than pieces of hard cardboard and paper that had fallen among the scrap metal? I looked along the immense, empty avenue, still wintry although summer was nearly upon us; a badly lit avenue, because there were hardly any vehicles, and it wasn't downtown. At that hour it would even be hard to find a cab, and what traffic there was seemed to rise from the asphalt, like a school of dolphins swimming silently on liquid cement. I got back home with none of the sense of peace my outings usually produced, but the same idea that had obsessed me the night before, the notion that I'd been walking through one of my roommate's maps. I scarcely slept.

The following day I was incapable of doing any decent work. I couldn't concentrate, wanting to finish everything as quickly as possible. I was beginning to understand why the story of Susana's madness had been so fascinating, and why, as a result, I was completely uninterested in her *real* past. I called Germán and told him my roommate needed to transport her collages and maps to the gallery.

"I called her last night," he said.

I was annoyed. Wasn't Susana just an acquaintance? Why all this familiarity?

"Ah," I responded.

"Are you OK?"

"I'm not sure,"

"Are you taking the drugs the psychiatrist prescribed?"

"Yes. And they were working until a while ago."

"So what's changed?"

"I don't know."

"Do you want me to come around tonight?"

"No. Let's talk tomorrow. Don't worry. I slept badly."

I hung up and didn't think any more about Germán. When I started work on the book, the widow's words formed tortuous threads, like hedges whose branches I had to prune, and as I continued with that task, it seemed what I saw on the screen were not individual letters but very precise drawings. I didn't care what I wrote, just allowed myself to be guided by the conversation between the letters and those drawings, certain that if I achieved a level of perfection in the threads, the union of form and content would be superb. That conviction kept me focused on my work until late. I didn't even stop to eat.

Susana arrived at the apartment carrying three bags of clothes.

"Come and see what I've bought," she said, draping a black satin dress over the sofa, plus a pair of harem pants and a couple of retro blouses. From a gold-colored box she extracted a pair of silver ballet flats with patent leather toe-caps, and from another a pair of Converse sneakers. She had also purchased a leopard-print jacket and a checked vest. "I don't usually celebrate before the event, but I really felt I deserved a reward," she continued. "And if it doesn't work out with the gallery, I'll be just as happy, or at least I guess I will. It's been two years since I bought any clothes. And I'm superstitious, I feel like I have to wear something new to make everything go well."

The clothes Susana had bought were a break from her usual severe, uninspiring style. They were the sorts of clothes I might have bought. I thought they showed bad taste. I wondered if I'd ever really been capable of interpreting her tendency to construct herself from movies, books, and TV series, or her silence about her work. Susana never behaved in a way you would expect from someone for whom things never worked out, who had never gotten anything she wanted from life, who as she approached fifty was still living in an unenviably precarious situation. What had seemed to me irritating and outlandish about her—and had made me think she was younger than her actual age—was what I also admired, because her behavior was a form of resistance. However, the sight of her showing off her new clothes shook that faith. Maybe Susana had never sought to be different, to survive, to resist, and I was just interpreting her through categories that only applied to me. And had I ever in fact admired her? Wasn't I perhaps seriously worried about ending up like her, and now, when she seemed on the point of *triumph*, of turning her life around, was I just idealizing her past to refute her present? As I formulated those ideas, I was also aware of their lack of utility; they were not the cause of my profound anxiety. What was getting in the way was Fabio—the absolute, cheerful, morose intrusion—and I was in no mood for that. Susana put on the silver shoes; her feet were like two spaceships designed to transport her through the air to the gallery. She tried on the leopard-skin jacket and the vest so I could admire how well they went with simple white blouses, like the one she was wearing. Then she seemed to realize time was pressing and started organizing her work into files and boxes. I felt the same rage as when she'd settled herself into the apartment. On the day she arrived, she'd left her suitcase in the bedroom with a few of her belongings, and then disappeared for a week. I couldn't bear that self-sufficiency. Day after day I'd waited for her to return, with all the rooms tidy.

Since my deadline was looming, I should have worked on the widow's book, but felt I needed to put distance between myself and Susana. I went out.

I'd decided I wasn't going to be caught unaware, and so when I heard the roar of the engine, I knew it must be them and ducked. The projectile bounced off a wall and fell to the ground. This time it was a cardboard bunny; I picked it up to get a better look. I was in a relatively unfamiliar area of Usera. When I tired of roaming around there, I crossed Pradolongo and then Avenida de los Poblados, until I reached a street whose name caused me that lightbulb moment of forgotten evidence: Calle del Plan Parcial, reached by crossing a couple of stretches of spongy lawn. Once again I could see cables running from upper floors to a streetlight, syphoning off its power without the least attempt to disguise the crime. A number of window frames were lined with sheets of plastic, which meant that in order to occupy the house the squatters had had to climb ladders and break the glass. Then I doubted that hypothesis. As on previous occasions, I came to the conclusion that those squats had the blessing of local inhabitants and the police. The buildings didn't look particularly old, but they also weren't dilapidated public housing. When in such areas, it was second nature to me to look for signs that I wasn't wrong. I crossed the park onto Primitiva Gañán; while carrying out my investigation it occurred to me that the postwar writer who was the subject of the widow's book would never have imagined that the city would expand to include the point where I was standing at that moment. In the past there had only been orchards, vegetable gardens, small dairy farms on this stretch of asphalt. This thought came to me like a revelation; I told myself that information had been planted in my mind by the postwar writer, his gaze passing over the whole of Madrid, observing its poorly thought-out growth. I asked his ghost where else I should look for squats to confirm my theory of the existence of another city.

I reached a street of old houses, and then took the metro and got out in a recently constructed area where the public housing was architect designed. I moved along the avenues looking carefully at those non-brick buildings. There were a few detached houses like shipping containers. I began to feel afraid; it seemed to me that this district zoned for residential use had been left to its own devices, since there was no uniformity in the final design details. I walked back to the apartment, arriving at three in the morning, and slept for an hour before beginning work on the widow's book. Susana got up at dawn: I'd never seen her in pajamas before.

"Is something wrong?" she asked.

"I've got a deadline for this book, and I've been working all night," I told her.

When she left, I went back to bed. Germán was coming

later and I wouldn't be fit to be seen. I got up at lunchtime without having slept a wink, and hid the widow's book so Susana wouldn't realize I hadn't met the deadline. Feeling I needed to smarten myself up, I tried on the clothes I'd inherited from my mother after her death: her tailored suits that made me look older, her long skirts, her fitted pants, her blazers. Elegant clothes don't do anything for me. I finally put on a red dress and waited for Susana on the sofa. Looking upward, I discovered some of the bugs from our shoes had formed small colonies in the corners of the ceiling. At six, Susana and Germán came in together.

"Don't you have to work?" asked Susana.

"I've been waiting to help you both."

Germán sat down next to me.

"Elisa, are you feeling OK?"

"Yes."

"Antidepressants sometimes have strange side effects. You're probably a bit out of it."

"I spent the whole night working, and I've just gotten back from the publisher's. I had a deadline. Aren't we going to load the car, then?"

I went to Susana's bedroom and grabbed a box. Germán did the same. The three of us made several trips to the car; I did my best to block out their conversation, but it was impossible, as they chatted and joked the whole time. It seemed like they knew each other very well. When the trunk was full, Germán folded down the seats and continued loading.

"You'll have to wait for us. There's no room to sit in the back," he said.

"Goodbye," I mumbled.

"I'll come back for you, and the three of us can have a drink when Susana's finished in the gallery. No way you're going to wait here in your red dress."

The engine sparked to life with a noise like a food processor.

When I got back inside the apartment my cell phone started ringing; it was Germán. I didn't answer. I knew that would mean he'd return for me more quickly, so I left the phone on my bed and went out. It was early evening. Not the hour for bumping into the guys from the truck, or walking deserted streets. The terrace cafés were buzzing with people anticipating summer, and there was a smell of Popsicles and vanilla ice cream. My plan was to go to the park in San Isidro to watch the gray twilight fall over the city. I'd done that before; it was a beautiful sight, completely without mystery. I made this effort because the urban sectors I now frequented held no more secrets. I did it to cling to what was literal.

Two years before, I'd been invited to a wedding in Manzanares. I enjoyed the bus journey through the snub-nosed scenery of La Mancha, and when I arrived I was in the mood to equally enjoy that historic town. I'd made a reservation at a small hotel in the center, and thought I would have no difficulty finding it, so when I left the bus station I asked the assistant at a deli for directions. She either got the address mixed up or, more likely, her explanation was unclear. It was noon, and hot, with that scorching, tree-less Castilian steppe heat; the architecture on the outskirts of town was insipid, and there wasn't a person in sight. I walked for a long time, until I reached an intersection that must have marked a point of inflection in my ever-greater certainty that I was going the wrong way. The intersection was not the point of inflection for anything, and I was no longer appreciating the scenery, no longer inventing stories about it, because the heat was unbearable, and I'd spent forty-five minutes with the sun beating down on me, and the weight of my wheel-less suitcase was making my back ache. It would have been impossible not to mention those simple facts if I had been asked for an impression of the town; the same thing happened with Susana.

I returned to the apartment at one in the morning. To kill time, I'd gone into a movie theater. I guessed that Susana and Germán would have come back to collect me, waited a few hours, and probably been both worried and annoyed. It hadn't occurred to me they would still be there, and even less in that state: lying naked on the sofa, Germán's head resting on my roommate's thigh. As they were asleep, I said nothing. On the table was my now-empty bottle of Polish vodka, plus the Orujo the monk from Burgos had given me. I picked up the Orujo and returned it to the chest. Then I went to my room and closed the door. Not long afterward, Germán knocked. He was dressed. He uttered a few variations on "We thought you weren't coming back," "We were worried," and then, taking courage from my expectant attitude, a rush of language, of thought, jostled on his tongue: "We wanted to celebrate," "I slept with Susana years ago; it wasn't a problem." The atmosphere reeked of alcohol and rolling tobacco.

"You don't have to explain," I said.

That was true only because it had been so in the past.

Germán used to tell me who he was sleeping with if it was relevant and, after parties, I'd seen him start the day in one of the girls' rooms. He didn't go looking for it, but when the suggestion came up, he had no objection to ending up in someone's arms. I'd only known him to have one stable relationship. That morning he was so drunk he dropped onto the bed and almost immediately fell asleep, muttering, "Sorry." I found this pathetic, and a consolation. When I looked into the living room, Susana had disappeared, but not without first clearing the table and opening the window. I lay down next to Germán. One thing felt like a relief: this would give me an excuse to ask her to leave, to have the pleasure of seeing that imagined past that was present in my apartment exit through the door. It gave me the excuse I needed to enter Susana's room, shake her shoulders, politely say, "I'd like you to move out tomorrow, please." Susana reduced to a mere bag of skin, to the stranger she already was.

Germán woke me at seven.

"I want to talk to you before I go to work," he blurted out, filling the space between his mouth and mine with vodka fumes.

When I opened my eyes, I felt as if I'd slept soundly, with an unusual, obfuscating depth; I was annoyed to be woken, to have to battle with the arid life my dreams had been an escape from. Or that's how it seemed in the brief moments of serenity that accompanied the dawn. I'd often had compensatory dreams in the past; they were no big deal, but did help me get things off my chest. Before I started talking the pills, my anxiety had been making a mockery of that restorative blackout.

I sat up; out of modesty, I'd slept in pajamas, and the unaccustomed weight of the cotton fabric felt wearisome. I took my pills, slipped on a light wrap, and left the room. Susana's alarm clock was ringing.

"You're angry," said Germán.

He had followed me out; his attitude was calming. He had a lousy hangover, and I couldn't help but imagine a failed fuck with my roommate. Or maybe they had done it before getting drunk.

"I'm going to tell Susana I want her to move out of the apartment," I told him.

"Can you afford that?"

"If you come to live here, yes. Or if you let me move into your place. Would you mind going now? I won't have the courage to tell her if you're here."

I didn't stop to consider what I'd just said. I was certain he would either move here to Aluche with me, or find space for me in his uncluttered apartment, with its high ceilings and laminate flooring, on Calle de la Luna, just north of the Gran Vía. I put the coffeepot on the stove. Susana was moving around in her room. When she came out, still naked but carrying a change of underwear and a towel, she looked at me with a coldness I didn't judge to be aggressive; rather, it was the result of haste and sleepiness. The result of a reality that still hadn't gelled, that you could still give the finger to. I made myself some tea; when Susana came out of the bathroom, by then fully awake, her expression had changed.

"Can you spare a moment?" I asked.

"I need to be out in fifteen minutes."

"There's coffee on the stove."

She filled one of the glasses we use for water to the brim and sat down across from me. Her damp hair had a pleasant, fruity smell. I felt grimy in my pajamas and robe, the traces of sleep still on my face.

"It's not because of yesterday, or not exactly. But I want you to move out. This seems like a good opportunity to tell you."

Susana's expression didn't change. Her mind was somewhere else; her body was simply obeying commands that had the power to resonate in our ears like an outmoded expression: Jumpin' Jehosaphat.

"Yes, it is," she said, making an effort to evaluate my position without condescension. "My hangover's making me a bit dopey."

She hesitated, as if she had no right to explain herself, but equally was unable not to rejoice in her triumph, or perhaps her luck, since she hadn't gone looking for anything. All she'd done was slip in through my inertia. I asked about her visit to the gallery; let her commence to make up for all her years of floundering. That was the most I could give Susana for a long time.

It took her less than two weeks to find a new apartment. Germán and I helped her move. Her mind was completely occupied by her forthcoming exhibition. The day she left, she brought me a bunch of tulips, and gave me one of the maps. It was a sly farewell. I was left with the fear that her departure didn't involve any form of closure.

PART THREE

INQUIRIES

"You've told me that after you moved in with Germán, you decided to continue believing in a sort of conspiracy theory."

"That's right, I was still looking around for signs of it when we went to live in an apartment we found in Prosperidad. It meant I had to wander around new neighborhoods. That unknown territory gave me an excuse; I could gather clues. Though during the day I pretended to myself it wasn't happening."

"I don't understand why, in your book, you take it for granted that the reader knows what's going on between Germán and the main character."

"He told me it was a sort of desperate attempt to attract my attention. He'd gotten drunk enough to be sure he wouldn't manage a hard-on. He didn't do anything with my roommate, just strip down. And to make me even angrier, he'd drunk the liquor I kept in the chest. He knows a lot of things about me. We've known each other for ten years."

"And now he's your partner."

"But Germán isn't the problem."

"As we progress with the sessions, you'll realize the problem may not lie where you think it does."

"OK."

"There's no mention of your employment situation at the end of your text, and that was the trigger for your crisis."

"It settled down, or rather it went back to a sort of stable instability. But they did pay what was outstanding. Carmentxu had a seizure and resigned. She got us all together, and said it was her work that had made her ill. That's probably true, though she didn't take care of herself either. She used to eat, drink, and smoke to excess. They replaced her with a Frenchman who's now my boss, and who happens to be very handsome. His name is Claude. I'm not sure if he's only there because he's got connections; I guess so, because he doesn't speak Spanish very well, he's not bilingual, and so can't judge our work. But I don't let it get to me. Germán earns more than me; his salary is enough to pay the rent. I'm accepting fewer commissions, and I've had time to write the novel. It's taken me to another place. Another mental space. I guess later on I'll have to face the employment situation again, but for the moment I've put it on the back burner."

"You say you've gotten over your, shall we say, hallucinations, but you want to tape our meetings to use as a sort of coda to the novel, and so set the cure down on paper. On the first day you told me that text you wrote years ago had triggered your crisis, and you wanted to put your therapeutic process on the record, in a literary sense, to ensure you would never stand on the verge of an abyss again. Isn't there a new fantasy hidden behind that?"

"I'd call it superstition."

"In your novel, you say you're not superstitious."

"What's in my novel is a character based on me, but it's not me. And the narrative isn't exact. I've tried to approach something, but maybe what I've actually done is quite different. The book isn't finished, and our meetings are part of it. I need to round it out. And I can't invent an ending. It turns out false. In fiction everything is false, but I'm not referring to that type of falsity—I mean not respecting the coherence of the text. So to maintain the coherence of what I've written, I need this conversation to take place."

"And is it more important for you to set down what happens in my office in order to finish off your book, or to be cured?"

"I'm not sure I understand you."

"I'll put it another way. What if we don't succeed in curing you? Would you write about that failure?"

"If I don't manage to get over the impression of being about to go out of my mind, that could be the last sentence of the book. Because to go on if nothing happens would be redundant, wouldn't it?"

NOTES

The text introducing the second part of this book was published in "El Cuaderno de Verano" in the newspaper *Público* on August 5, 2010, under the title "Un ejemplo deplorable de escritura circular."

The quotation on page 23 ("specter of thought") is from Vladimir Nabokov's *Transparent Things*, originally published by Weidenfeld & Nicolson in 1972, although I in fact read it in an article by Enrique Vila-Matas entitled "Los viajes andados" in *El País* on November 13, 2012.